"You will spend many an hour just laughing
through her books."*

**Praise for
the Undead novels of MaryJanice Davidson**

"Delightful, wicked fun!" —Christine Feehan

"A lighthearted vampire pastiche that recalls the work of
Charlaine Harris." —*Omaha World-Herald*

"Chick lit meets vampire action in this creative, sophisti-
cated, sexy and wonderfully witty book."
—Catherine Spangler

"A laugh-a-minute book." —*Romance Junkies*

"Davidson delivers more wildly witty, irreverent and just
plain funny adventures in her patently hilarious style."
—*Romantic Times* (4½ stars)

"One of the funniest, most satisfying series to come along
lately. If you're [a] fan of Sookie Stackhouse and Anita
Blake, don't miss Betsy Taylor. She rocks."
—*The Best Reviews*

"I don't care what mood you are in, if you open this book
you are practically guaranteed to laugh . . . top-notch humor and a fascinating perspective of the vampire world."
—*ParaNormal Romance Reviews*

"[A] wickedly clever and amusing romp. Davidson's witty
dialogue, fast pacing, smart plotting, laugh-out-loud humor and sexy relationships make this a joy to read."
—*Booklist*

And don't miss
Jennifer Scales and the Ancient Furnace
by MaryJanice Davidson and Anthony Alongi

Sleeping
with the
Fishes

MaryJanice Davidson

JOVE BOOKS, NEW YORK

THE BERKLEY PUBLISHING GROUP
Published by the Penguin Group
Penguin Group (USA) Inc.
375 Hudson Street, New York, New York 10014, USA
Penguin Group (Canada), 90 Eglinton Avenue East, Suite 700, Toronto, Ontario M4P 2Y3, Canada
(a division of Pearson Penguin Canada Inc.)
Penguin Books Ltd., 80 Strand, London WC2R 0RL, England
Penguin Group Ireland, 25 St. Stephen's Green, Dublin 2, Ireland (a division of Penguin Books Ltd.)
Penguin Group (Australia), 250 Camberwell Road, Camberwell, Victoria 3124, Australia
(a division of Pearson Australia Group Pty. Ltd.)
Penguin Books India Pvt. Ltd., 11 Community Centre, Panchsheel Park, New Delhi—110 017, India
Penguin Group (NZ), Cnr. Airborne and Rosedale Roads, Albany, Auckland 1310, New Zealand
(a division of Pearson New Zealand Ltd.)
Penguin Books (South Africa) (Pty.) Ltd., 24 Sturdee Avenue, Rosebank, Johannesburg 2196,
South Africa

Penguin Books Ltd., Registered Offices: 80 Strand, London WC2R 0RL, England

SLEEPING WITH THE FISHES

A Jove Book / published by arrangement with the author

PRINTING HISTORY
Jove mass-market edition / December 2006

Copyright © 2006 by MaryJanice Alongi.
Excerpt from *Undead and Uneasy* by MaryJanice Davidson copyright © 2006 by MaryJanice Alongi.
Cover design by Judith Lagerman.
Text design by Kristin del Rosario.

ISBN: 0-515-14222-0

JOVE®
Jove Books are published by The Berkley Publishing Group,
a division of Penguin Group (USA) Inc.,
375 Hudson Street, New York, New York 10014.
JOVE is a registered trademark of Penguin Group (USA) Inc.
The "J" design is a trademark belonging to Penguin Group (USA) Inc.

PRINTED IN THE UNITED STATES OF AMERICA

10 9 8 7 6 5 4 3 2 1

For my husband, who did tons of research for this project, who came up with countless ways to turn the mermaid genre on its head, who helped me several steps of the way with this book, who supports me in the good times and bad, and who loves that I make more money than he does.

Acknowledgments

I knew next to nothing about the things in this book when Fred popped into my head. Oh, sure, I knew about mermaid clichés and stereotypes (Ariel, of Disney-movie fame, yowling on top of a rock in a harbor instantly springs to mind) but nothing about the U.S. Coast Guard, marine biology, sea life, the National Ocean Service or the New England Aquarium. (I'm from land-locked Minnesota.)

All these places and subjects had extensive books and websites available, which were truly a godsend to this landlubber. And I *did* have my wedding reception at the New England Aquarium years ago, which helped.

Further, I must (again) thank my editor, Cindy Hwang. I made the gross mistake of initially writing Fred the Mermaid in first person—gross because first person should be used sparingly, if at all, and a mistake because Fred ended up sounding like Betsy with fins.

Even worse, it took me two hundred pages to figure that out. So, seconds from my deadline, I ripped the whole thing up and started over: page one, chapter one. Cindy, to her great credit, did not implode, burst into tears, quit, tear up my contract, hire a hit man, smack me upside the head or even raise her voice. She just cheerfully extended my deadline and asked me to be sure to tell her if I needed anything else.

Little did she know, my grandfather was going to die three weeks later. Again: no weeping (well, there was weeping, but it was all on my end), no threats, nothing but calm condolence and an assurance that the last thing I should worry about is some silly deadline. (She managed to say this without ripping out any of her hair as she pictured the fall line with a big hole where *Sleeping with the Fishes* was going to be.)

Thus, an even later manuscript. (See, see? Unlike most writers, I'll actually admit it: the book was late. It was entirely my fault. I suck.) And, though she must have been sorely tempted, rather than shoot the thing straight to galleys, the same team of editors descended on the book and did their usual stellar job of fixing my mistakes and making me look all, y'know, smart 'n' stuff. These people turned a messy pile of mistake-ridden pages (more than a few, tear-splotched) into a book, the one you're holding in your hands.

It's people like me who give people like her peptic ulcers. I'll get the credit and hardly anyone will know her name: Cindy Hwang. People will wait in line for my autograph and they'll ask her where the bathroom is.

Fair? No. The saving of me? Good God, yes.

Author's Note

As a landlubber, I could only rely on my imagination so much. Various sources were invaluable. The World Wide Web is truly a wonderful place:

http://www.wellesley.edu/Psychology/Cheek/Narrative/home.html

http://life.bio.sunysb.edu/marinebio/becoming.html

http://oceanlink.island.net/career/career2.html

http://www.uscg.mil/USCG.shtm

http://www.uscgboating.org

http://www.legislative.noaa.gov/noaainyourstate/massachusetts.html

This is the part where I write something banal like, "There's no such thing as vampires," or whatever. And I was in the middle of typing, "Of course there's no such thing as mermaids," but after all the research and time put into this book and all the stories I heard and . . . well, I wonder.

Let's just say Fred is one of a kind and leave it at that.

Sleeping

with the

Fishes

O, train me not, sweet mermaid, with thy note,
To drown me in thy sister's flood of tears:
Sing, siren, for thyself and I will dote:
Spread o'er the silver waves thy golden hairs,
And as a bed I'll take them and there lie.

> —WILLIAM SHAKESPEARE, *Comedy of Errors*

In the blue depth of the waters,
Where the wave hath no strife,
Where the wind is a stranger,
And the sea-snake hath life,
Where the Mermaid is decking
Her green hair with shells;
Like the storm on the surface
Came the sound of thy spells.

> —LORD BYRON, "Manfred"

At sea once more we had to pass the Sirens, whose sweet singing lures sailors to their doom. I had stopped up the ears of my crew with wax, and I alone listened while lashed to the mast, powerless to steer toward shipwreck.

—HOMER, *The Odyssey*

Them sirens loved him up and turned him into a horny toad!

—*O Brother, Where Art Thou?*

Yeah . . . bullshit.

—FREDRIKA BIMM, HYBRID MERMAID

One

§

The unbelievable horror began when Fred walked in on her parents making love on the living room coffee table. Like all children (even when grown), her first muddled impression was that her father was hurting her mother. Or perhaps fixing her back. Her second impression was that the coffee-table books (*Alaska: The Last Frontier*; *Cape Cod: An Explorer's Guide*; *The Black Sea: A History*) must sting like hell on her mother's knees. Her third impression sounded something like this:

"Aaaaeeeiiiiieeee!"

Her mother slipped and National Geographic's *Seals of the Antarctic* flew like a tiddly wink from the coffee table and hit the floor with a thud. Her father flinched but, unfortunately, did not fall off (or out of) her mother.

Fred darted across the room and, before she realized what she was doing, hauled her father off and tossed him over the back of the couch. She then yanked the puke-orange throw from said couch and threw it over her mother.

"Ow," her father groaned from out of sight.

Her mother wriggled under the throw, sat up, and faced her daughter, her normally pale face flushed with wrath. Or something else Fred did not want to think about. "Fredrika Bimm, what do you think you're doing?"

"Freaking out. Losing my mind. Thinking about snapping your husband's spine. Squashing the urge to vomit. Wishing I'd died at childbirth."

"Oh, you say that when you don't get a prize in your Lucky Charms," her mother snapped. "What's your problem, miss? You don't knock anymore?" Her mother, a good-looking blonde with silver streaks and shoulder-length hair (and a disturbingly sweaty face), climbed off the coffee table with remarkable dignity, fastened the blanket to cover her chubby thighs, and went around the couch to help her husband. "You just barge in?"

"I have a key, I didn't barge," Fred pointed out, still revolted but regretting the violence. "And you told me to come over."

"Yesterday. I told you to come over yesterday."

"I was working," Fred tried not to whine, or stare. "I couldn't just ditch all the fish. Although they deserve it, the little bastards. Anyway, I couldn't come."

"Well," her mother retorted, "neither could I."

Fred again tried not to vomit, and succeeded for the moment. She peered over the couch, where her father was groaning and clutching the small of his back. His bald spot was flushed almost purple. His ponytail had come undone. "Sorry, Dad."

"Sorry, hell," he gasped. "I swear, I'll never touch her again."

3

"Oh, Sam, just stop it."

"Not even if we're married for another thirty years."

Fred flashed a rare smile. "Okay."

"Fred, stop it! You, too, Sam." Mrs. Bimm helped her husband to his feet and hustled him out of the living room. Then she turned on her daughter.

"Fredrika."

"Mom, put yourself in my fins."

"Fredrika Shea Bimm."

"Mom, he was *fucking my mother*. He's a mother-fucker! What would you have done?"

"Not tossed him halfway across the room," her mother snapped, then puffed her bangs out of her face. "What in the world is wrong with you? You're almost thirty, for heaven's sake."

"And you're almost fifty! Way too old to be—to be—yech."

Her mother stuck a stubby finger in Fred's face. Everything about Moon Bimm was short and stubby, compared to Fred's long lankiness. Even Fred's nose was long, and while Mrs. Bimm's mouth was perma-

4

nently turned up in a smile, Fred's everyday expression was a scowl. If Fred hadn't seen the birth certificate, she would have doubted any birth relation to Moon Bimm. "Violence. Language. Manners. All unacceptable."

"I overreacted, okay? I'm sorry, all right?"

"Not to me. To your father. Who is probably icing his back right this minute."

"Hopefully he's put some pants on first."

Fred looked around the small living room, which was artfully decorated in Cape Cod Tourist. "Why here, Mom? Why next to the pleather chair? The La-Z-Boy? Why not anywhere else?" *Why not never? Never ever?* "I mean . . . you've got a bed."

"We are often strongly affected in the living room," her mother said primly, then giggled (giggled! *O gods of all the seas, kill me now and make it snappy*) and marched out, trailing blanket fuzz behind her.

"Oh, fucking gross," Fred muttered, following her mother.

Two

🌊

"It's not as bad as you think, Fred," the Defiler of Her Mother said, wincing when he moved the bag of frozen peas to better cover his lower back. He had, thankfully, put on pants. Said frozen peas were stuffed in back of said pants. Fred's mom was still prancing around in the couch blanket, all "nature's never wrong" and "be empowered, not embarrassed" and "you shouldn't cover up God's handiwork."

Is there anything sillier than a grown-up hippie?

"I'm sorry you had to catch us in an intimate moment—"

"Bird-watching Wednesday," her mother said solemnly, then giggled again.

Fred groaned and looked around for a fork or a spoon or a gravy boat to gouge out her eyes. And ears. Because Moon Bimm was referring to the cardinal tattooed on her left butt cheek. Other mothers had laugh lines and wrinkles. Not animal tattoos.

She rested her forehead on her hands, her green hair brushing the table. She stared at the kelp-colored strands and thought, *That's it. I'm running away for sure. Again. Twenty-nine-year-olds run away all the time. It's perfectly normal. It's—*

"Why," she muttered, "did you call me over in the first place?" *And why didn't I come yesterday, when she actually called?*

"Oh, that. Well . . ." Her mother fluttered about the kitchen, strands of the couch blanket making her look like a freaked-out caterpillar. "We believe—your father and I believe—that is, Sam and I believe in full disclosure."

"So I see," Fred sniffed, eyeing the blanket.

"Lies and deception, they're a bad trip, honey. A baaaa—"

"You want to talk bad trips? Cast your mind back, Mom. Your acid-fried mind. Remember ten minutes ago?"

Moon Bimm ignored her daughter's sarcasm; she'd had almost three decades of practice. "Lies and deception, baby. They can make you physically ill. There's science to back this up, hon. People get ulcers and high blood pressure, just from keeping secrets! And—"

"Mom. Will you cut to it, please? I have to go home and Clorox my eyeballs."

"We're going to adopt."

Fred kept staring at her hands.

"Hon? Did you hear me?"

"If you're adopting, why are you fucking?"

"Language," her father said, squirming on the chair and groping for the bag of peas.

Moon "Children Should Be Allowed to Express Themselves However They Wish" Bimm focused on the sentiment, not the verbiage. "So lovemaking is only for procreation?"

"When it's your *mother* and your *father*, yes, lovemaking is only for procreation!" Fred screamed. She longed to toss the kitchen table through the dining room hutch. "I have seen some dark and wicked things, Mom and Dad, take it from me—you would not believe what lurks in the oceans' deep. I have seen a shark barf out another shark and then eat it again. But nothing I've seen was as bad as my mother and father—"

"Except I'm not your father," her father said.

"—as my mother and father—uh—doing dark and wicked things in the ocean. What?"

"Full disclosure," her mother said, dramatically swooping about the kitchen, blanket flapping. "All this paperwork we have to fill out for the adoption, it got me thinking. And it's time you knew the truth. Sam Bimm isn't your biological father."

"Yeah, Mom. I know."

Her mom sat down across from her and took Fred's cold (they were always cold) hands in her warm ones.

Even now, Fred took comfort from her mother's touch: how many times had those hands tucked her in, held her, rubbed her back? Her mom was like a walking, talking, jasmine-scented electric blanket.

"I know it'll take some getting used to," she said with touching earnestness. "And I'm sorry you had to live with the lie."

"Mom. I know Sam isn't my father."

"And I'm so sorry I kept it from you!" Moon's hands plunged into her blonde hair and made fists; for a minute she looked like a seventies version of Mad Ophelia. "But there was a stigma, especially back then, and I couldn't go home and even though it was perfectly natural, even though it's what my body is for and it was beautiful and amazing, I was ashamed."

"A shamed hippie?" Fred wondered aloud.

"And then there was Sam—"

"So, even worse problems?" Fred guessed.

Her mother frowned and continued. "And I was so happy to see him again and he—"

"—had a thing for knocked-up blondes who puked in the morning?"

"Fred, I don't think you're—"

"Mom. I appreciate you getting this off your chest and all—" Fred tried not to stare at her mother's boobs. Fred wished the woman would get something *on* her chest, like a turtleneck. "But I had that one figured out by the time I was five. Not, by the way, that it makes it any easier to pretend his tongue wasn't where it was ten minutes ago. But yeah, I knew."

"You did?" Sam asked, shifting uneasily as pea water started to trickle down his butt crack.

"Dad. Sam. Whatever. Look at you. Look at me. I'm a mermaid and you couldn't get a membership at the Y."

Her mother threw up her hands. The blanket gaped. Fred stared at the ceiling. "And how such a wondrous creature can have such silly hang-ups is beyond—"

"Mom, ask anybody on the planet: would it weird you out to walk in the front door and see your mom on all fours? I guarantee—mermaid, human, blue whale, marmoset, pixie, leprechaun, zombie—they'll all say yes." She turned to her squirming father.

11

"Remember that time you panicked in the tide pool and I had to get you out? I was seven, Dad, and the water was only up to my knees."

"There were *things* in there," Sam said, shuddering at the memory.

"Yeah, Sam. Minnows. It was the fourth or fifth time I'd had to save you, and I'd never had a swimming lesson in my life. Also, you have brown eyes and mine are the color of brussels sprouts. Also, you have—had—brown hair and mine's the color of the ocean. Also, you never grow a tail and you're right-handed; while I'm—did you get this?—a *mermaid* and a *lefty*!"

"No need to scream," Mom sniffed.

"I hate it when you treat me like I'm freaking stupid."

"Nobody thinks you're freaking stupid," her mom soothed in her "I think my kid's freaking stupid" voice. "Everyone in this room is a living creature deserving of our love and respect."

"If you try to hold my hand and make a nurture circle," Fred warned, "I will kill you."

Three

🐚

Unfortunately for Fred and her sanity, the night-mare wasn't over yet. Her mother, gripped with the mania of truth-telling, coughed up the whole sordid story.

It seemed Moon Bimm (née Moon Westerberg) had been putzing around on Chapin Beach, Cape Cod, with a bunch of her idiot hippie friends, high on pot and *le Gallo Jug*, lonesome and wondering what it all meant, got separated from her pot-smoking, Gallo-swigging pals (which Fred would have thought a relief, but Moon didn't agree), and ran into a suave, green-eyed fellow and was *so fucking drunk she didn't notice he was half fish.*

"But if he was a merman, how did you—whoa. Whoa. Forget it. I can't believe, in light of recent hideous events, that I even asked you that. Do not answer. Do *not* answer. We are at DEFCON 3 and rising. We—"

"Oh, just stop it, you big baby." Her mother stretched her neck to squint at Fred's exasperated features. "Why you can't understand how beautiful and natural sex can be and why you have so many Puritan hang-ups about it—how a child of mine can be so—"

"Mom, now's not the time for the 'Peace and Lurrrv' lecture."

"He had legs like you do, of course," she said, completely ignoring Fred's emphatic backpedaling five seconds earlier. "I imagine he can grow a tail or not, as he likes. As you like." Moon frowned. "I guess any mer-person can. I thought you could do it or not because you were half human. But unless he was also half human—"

"That'd be super duper for him. So he jumps your drunken bones, you have sand-pillow talk, then he leaps into the sea and disappears? So you're telling me . . . what? My real father's an asshole? And you're a slut? Because he owes you for years of child support payments, that's one. And two—"

"Must you always label people?"

"Must you shovel truth down my throat?"

"As I was saying," Moon went on with admirable dignity, considering recent events and what she was hardly wearing, "ten months later and there you were."

"*Ten* months?" How had she never done the math before? Easy. Her mom had never talked about her father—her real father—before. Just "oh and we met and got married because society will insist on that silly piece of paper and we've been a family ever since."

And Fred, knowing her mother would answer anything—*anything*—was the only kid on the block who never went through the "where did I come from?" phase. Moon not only would have answered the question in disgusting and embarrassing detail, she would have surfed pornography websites with her daughter to investigate different methods.

"It takes longer for mer-people to gestate." Sam was looking at Fred thoughtfully. He taught Natural Science at 4C (Cape Cod Community College). "Or hybrids. Or—"

"So why'd you marry her, Sam? It was all Free Love and all the maryjane you could smoke and don't trust anyone over eighty back then."

"Thirty," her mother gurgled. "And marijuana? Wasn't on it. Poisons the body. Wine is bad enough." She winked at her daughter. "Look at the trouble three glasses of bad Chardonnay got me in!" Moon wouldn't take a Tylenol for a broken leg. Sadly, Fred knew this for a fact.

"Anyway—"

"No, no, that's enough," Fred broke in hastily. "I get it now. The gaping void inside me is complete, and filled with truth. No need to—"

"—your mother and I knew each other in high school, and went our separate ways after graduation.

When I ran into her, she was just as radiant and glowing as I remembered her."

"Probably all the puking," Fred suggested.

"And we fell in love and Sam loved you long before you were born. We both did. We loved . . . the *idea* of you." Her mom closed her eyes and took on a dreamy expression Fred knew well. "And the first time I gave you a bath and your legs grew together and your scales came down and you splashed me and broke the baby tub, I was so amazed—and so thrilled—"

"Girl turns into fish, news at eight?" Fred suggested. "Come on, Mom. You weren't a little freaked out?"

"I thought you were a miracle," she replied, and the simple dignity in her voice wiped the smirk off Fred's face. "I still do." She turned to Sam. "Thank goodness I had a natural childbirth right here in this house! Think of the mess if all kinds of Western medicine had descended on poor Fred!" She turned back to her daughter. "I was scared to even bring you in for your vaccinations. And I quit once we realized you couldn't ever get sick."

"Well." Fred coughed. "That's—ah. That's nice, Mom. A miracle. That's—miraculous. So that's why you called me over? To tell me stuff I already knew?"

"We didn't *know* you knew," Sam pointed out. "And as your mother said, filling out all the paperwork, and all the meetings, got us thinking."

"Why are you adopting?"

Her parents gave her puzzled "why not?" looks.

Fred tried to explain. "Most people your age would be thrilled to have the place to themselves."

"Well, I don't know if thrilled is exactly the—"

"Sam, you don't even have to work—you still get checks from your dad's invention, right?"

"Right." Sam's father had thought up edible underwear. The family got a piece of every fruit panty or chocolate G-string ever sold. "But we have all this space..." He gestured vaguely to the kitchen. "And it's such a nice location."

Real nice. Right on the ocean—Fred knew that the four-bedroom, three-bathroom "shack" on the bay would sell for a cool two-point-two if her parents ever wanted to move. But her "earth mother" mother took to Sam's money like a—well, like a fish to water. And they would never sell.

And even with all the donations to the Audubon Society and the YMCA and the Cape Cod Literary Council and the Hospice of Cape Cod and the Hyannis Public Library, there was still plenty left every year. Every month.

"And you've got your own life now," Sam still droned. "We hardly ever see you."

"Work. Keeps me busy," she mumbled.

"Honey, it wasn't a reprimand!"

"Sounded like one."

"You're a grown woman, you have your own life."

Ha.

"And we have ours and we're just not—we're not ready for it just to be the two of us yet." Her mother reached out, and Sam, as he always did, took her hand. "It just feels wrong."

Ah, her life. Her wonderful life. She'd last been on a real date six years ago, her boss kept trying to fix her up, the fish at work were deep in rebellion mode, and whatever way you looked at it she was a freak.

Freak. Abnormality. Anomaly. Glitch. Genetic hiccup.

And this was why her folks wanted another kid? Because they thought they did such a hot job on the first one?

Well, maybe it'd be fun to raise one that didn't grow a tail and pick fights with tuna.

"Okay, well, good luck and all." Fred paused, waiting for a response. When none was forthcoming, she continued. "If you need a reference from, uh, someone you raised, I can write a letter. Or whatever."

"That'd be lovely, Fred." Her mother hugged her. Fred stood stiffly for it, then sneezed when the blanket fuzz tickled her nose.

"Mom. Kleenex."

"Never mind. Oh, I feel so much better now that the whole story is out! Don't you feel better, baby?"

"Ecstatic."

Four

Before leaving, Fred took a dip in the indoor saltwater pool. She could have jumped in the ocean just outside the back door, but didn't feel like worrying about tourists. And it comforted her parents when she used it. Finally, it felt better than the ocean—no seaweed ready to entwine in her hair, no nosy codfish following her around, and she knew damn well the mercury levels in her own pool were just fine.

Point of fact, she preferred pools to the open sea.

The ocean was filled with horrors and fish shit. The pool was a controlled environment.

Now if she could just get a handle on those rotten angelfish at work—

That thought eventually propelled her back to her legs, and out of the pool, and into her clothes, and out the door. Her parents were nowhere to be found, meaning they had decamped to their bedroom and were finishing what Fred had interrupted.

Excellent. Well, not excellent, but she disliked good-byes, and her mom always acted like she was hitchhiking across Europe instead of driving to Boston.

With traffic, it was a ninety-minute drive to the Quincy T-stop, a twenty-minute ride to the Green Line, five minutes to the Blue, and then she popped out of the T at the New England Aquarium stop. It was late enough that she could hopefully slip in the employee entrance and get back to work without anybody—

"Dr. Bimm!"

Fuck.

She turned and beheld her boss, Dr. Barbara Robinson, a short woman with a blonde Valkyrie braid and almond-shaped brown eyes. Dr. Barb had her lab coat buttoned all the way to the top, as usual. Fred didn't even know where hers was.

Also as usual, Dr. Barb was trotting. Not walking fast, but almost running. She trotted everywhere: meetings, charity functions, feedings, seal shows. Fred couldn't imagine what the "kind of hurry" was. The fish weren't going anywhere. Neither were the tourists.

"Hi, Dr. Barb."

"Dr. Bimm, I'd like you to meet our new water fellow, Dr. Thomas Pearson. Dr. Pearson, this is Dr. Fredrika Bimm." She looked up at Pearson, blinking rapidly. "Dr. Bimm takes care of Main One for us."

"Fred," Fred said, sticking out her hand. "I keep the big fish from chomping on the little fish." She ignored Dr. Barb's wince. Dr. Barb liked full titles (yawn) and to make people's jobs sound more interesting than they were (double yawn). Fred's job was to jump into the four-story tank, toss dead smelt at

23

the fish and make sure the levels were good and the sea turtles didn't bully the sharks (sounded out of type, but it really happened on occasion). That was it. "Main One" indeed. The big freaking tank, that's what it was.

Dr. Pearson clasped her outstretched hand, winced at the chill (she didn't take it personally; everyone did), and shook it like a pepper shaker. "Hi there. Please call me Thomas."

"Muh," she replied. But then, he *was* gorgeous. Tall, really quite tall (she was lanky but he had a good three inches on her), with brown hair—except it wasn't just brown; even in the yucky fluorescent lighting she could see the gold and red highlights—cut short and neat. A lab coat, she noted disapprovingly; but then, he was new, and Dr. Barb probably wrestled him into it. Brown eyes—but again, not just brown. Brown with gold flecks. The flecks twinkled at her and sized her up at the same time. Strong nose. Swimmer's shoulders, long legs and narrow hips. And . . . dimples?

"—new to the area so I hope you'll help the NEA

family show him what a wonderful part of the country this is, particularly this time of year," Dr. Barb was yakking.

"Yeah," Fred said. *What was she talking about? What time of year is it?*

Dr. Barb must have interpreted the usual blank expression on Fred's face. "You know. New England in the fall, and all that."

"Um," she replied.

"Leaves changing? Autumn nip in the air? Kids going back to school, fresh beginnings?"

"Okay."

"Dr. Bimm. You had no idea it was September already, did you?"

"Not part of my job."

"Chatty, aren't you?" Thomas twinkled. There was no other word for it: he was grinning and his dimples were showing and his big dark eyes were shining and he was *twinkling* at her.

She shrugged.

"I love your hair," he said. "That's the most amazing green I've ever seen."

Dr. Barb frowned. "Dr. Bimm has blue hair."

Thomas shook his head. "No, it's the color of the grass on the first day of summer." He lowered his voice. "I write romance novels under the name Priscilla D'Jacqueline."

"You what?"

"But it's *blue*," Dr. Barb insisted.

"Um, shut up about my hair now?" Fred suggested.

"Right, right. Well, on with the tour." Dr. Barb started her hallway trot, dragging Thomas by the elbow. "Thank you for your time, Dr. Bimm. We'll leave you to your work."

"Okay."

"And don't forget to say hello to the new intern."

"I won't," she lied.

"It was nice to meet you, Fredrika!" he managed as he was dragged away.

"Not Fredrika. Fred. Not Dr. Bimm," she continued to the now-empty hallway. "Fred."

New water fellow. Yum.

After a moment's thought, she shoved Thomas out of her brain (he went fairly easily) and went back to work.

Tried to, anyway. On the way to her lab, she nearly collided with a creature of unspeakable evil and annoyance: an undergrad.

"Oh, hiiiiii!" the creature burbled, straightening her perfectly straight bangs and sticking out a small warm paw for Fred to shake. "Gosh, Dr. Bimm, right? Gosh! I'm super happy I have a chance to meet you! Yeah! Because I'm hoping to learn so much from you!" She laughed, as if the very idea was so exciting it could not be contained. "Yeah!"

Fred stared at the creature. She pegged the woman at about nineteen. Short—she came up to the middle of Fred's chest. Maybe—it was hard to tell from all the bouncing around she was doing. Elbow-length platinum blonde hair. No roots. A natural wave— almost a ripple—running through it, giving her hair bounce . . . unless it was the woman's actual bouncing that gave it bounce.

A flawless complexion, of course. Big, wide, blue eyes, of course, the color of the sky. A small, perfect nose. A small, pointed chin. Not a freckle or a pimple to be seen. A perfect little figure beneath the lab coat that (groan) Dr. Barb had no doubt made her wear.

Tiny (because of course her feet were small and comely), perfect high heels. Black, of course, because interning was a Serious Business.

"—and ohmigod I've wanted to work here since I—"

"Was a little girl."

"Ohmigod, yeah! Because I—"

"Loved dolphins."

"Yeah! Wow, they said you were, like, super smart or something but you're rilly rilly smart, like a genius! Yeah!"

"You're not," Fred asked with deep suspicion, "going to do a cheer or something, are you?"

"How did you know," Perfect Girl gasped, "that I was on the cheer team back home in Yarmouth?"

"I'm rilly rilly smart." Fred started backing away but Perfect Girl had taken that as an invitation to follow, and was stuck to Fred's side like a barnacle. "Why don't you, uh . . ."

"Dr. Barb said I should watch you and Dr. Pearson and Jamie and all the others on my first day to figure out where you need me."

"What if we don't need you?"

"Oh Dr. Bimm, you're rilly a riot! Ohmigod! Dr. Barb didn't tell me you were so funny!"

"Dr. Barb," Fred warned, "is in a world of trouble when I see her again."

"So ohmigod you're in charge of the big tank? You feed all the fish 'n' stuff?"

"Yes."

"But there's, like, gotta be more to it than that, right?" Perfect Girl tossed her hair. "Because just anybody could feed fish, right?"

"No, you pegged it. That's all there is to it. That's completely, totally all."

"Oh Dr. Bimm, you crack me up."

"I'd like to crack you up," she muttered.

"Ohmigod! I totally forgot." Again, she stuck out her hand. "I'm Madison Fehr."

"Fair?"

"No, F-E-H-R, but yeah, it's pronounced like that. And *Madison*. You know. *Madison*."

Fred sighed. "As in the mermaid from *Splash*?"

"Exactly!" Madison squealed. "I mean is that, like, all serendipitous or what? It totally totally is."

Fred was fairly certain she was rocketing toward an insulin reaction of some sort. She had to get away from this gibbering teenager before something terrible happened. To both of them.

"Well, it was nice to meet you, Madison, but I have to get back to work."

"Oh, can I come with you? It'd be rilly rilly neat to see you work!"

"No," Fred said, recoiling. "You can't."

"Well, poop." Madison pouted, then instantly recovered. "I guess I'll go see if I can learn the register in the gift shop, then."

"Swell."

"But if you change your mind and I can, like, help you, just let me know. I've, like, got my Scoobie certification and everything!"

"Scuba."

"What?"

"Self-Contained Underwater Breathing Apparatus. Scuba. Not Scoobie."

"Right! Anyway, I can do that. I totally totally can. So if you want some help, just page me and I'll come right over."

"The inverse of that would be if I don't page you, you'll stay far far away?"

"Ohmigod, you are so funny! Okay, nice to meet you, Dr. Bimm!" She was already trip-trapping away on her little heels, and waving over one shoulder. "Bye!"

For a long, awful moment, Fred thought she might gag. She got control over herself and actually managed a half-hearted wave back.

Five

🦄

While she was struggling into her scuba suit, and trying to mentally scour Madison from her brain, it occurred to Fred that Thomas had actually noticed her real hair color.

Which wouldn't be so unusual, except nobody had ever, ever noticed her hair was green except her mother. In fact, when she complained about it, about the teasing and the crude jokes from strangers ("Do your cuffs and collar match?") her mother had told her something silly and hippieish, to wit: "Your true love will be the man who truly sees you as you are."

Uh-huh, yank the other one, Mom.

But Thomas had not only seen, he had commented. Repeatedly. Even after being corrected by his new boss. And no crass jokes, either.

Her ridiculous hair was like the ocean: although it looked blue to most people it was, in reality, green. And dry as straw and fraught with split ends due to all the time she spent being wet, but that was another issue. And really, more her friend Jonas's problem than hers. *(Note to Fred,* she thought: *L'Oreal just isn't doing the job; time to try the Philosophy line.)*

She was finally in her suit, a swollen sausage in its casing, everything where it belonged, all the dumb tubes in place (one or two tourists might notice that she wasn't using a mask or oxygen tank), her fins on, the whole outfit useless and silly beyond belief and a *lie,* and she sat on the edge of the top level of the tank, at the very top floor of the NEA, and fell backward into Main One.

And flailed around uselessly and fought the urge to grow a tail, to be real

(fake)

and staggered through a small school of angelfish and thrashed past a nurse shark and almost knocked a sea turtle sprawling and accidentally swam upside-down for a few seconds until she got her bearings. Because she could not swim without her tail.

Just . . . couldn't. She had tried. She'd taken lessons for years. Moon had tried to teach her (what a disaster *that* had been).

It was no good. It was like her body knew she could grow a tail and fins and scales so what was the point of learning to swim with legs?

And so she couldn't.

She was a mermaid, employed as a marine biologist, who couldn't swim.

She was also a gainfully employed member of the New England Aquarium, charged with the care and feeding of the Main One inhabitants, who had forgotten the dead smelt.

Goddammit!

Well, the hell with it. She'd wait until everyone had gone home and then get the smelt. Nobody in the tank would starve to death if they had to wait another two or three hours. Instead she eyed the occupants of Main One and judged their health and overall appearance.

Everybody looked good. Unlike animals in zoos, fish tended to thrive in controlled environments. It was as though fish did well if they weren't constantly worrying about being chomped, and if the freedom of the open sea was what they gave up, it was a small price to pay.

Fred could relate.

A nurse shark swam lazily past her and she touched it with her mind. It wasn't any more difficult than adding double-digit numbers in her head.

You okay?

Hungry. Fish girl bring fish.

Yeah, well, so what else was new? Fish girl bring fish. Why not make it her new title, for the love of—

Something made her glance up and she looked through the windows of the tank and saw Thomas peering in at her, waving frantically.

Bemused, she waved a gloved hand back.

Six

"I know what you're thinking." Fred's best friend, Jonas Carrey, declared, sitting down opposite her. They were at their favorite window-side table at the Legal Sea Foods restaurant across from the NEA.

"I doubt that very much," she replied gloomily, stirring her strawberry margarita.

"You're thinking you're a freak, nobody understands you, you're a lone wolf in a pack of nutjobs, blah-blah." The waitress materialized and Jonas said, "An appletini, please."

"Oh, Jonas!" Fred practically yelled. "Those are so over."

"Hey. I'm secure enough in my sexuality to order any girlie drink in the world. Now tell me I'm right. Tell me I knew what you were thinking."

"I walked in on my folks doing it doggy style less than four hours ago."

"Waitress!" Jonas screamed, clicking his fingers madly. "Bring two!" Then, more quietly, "You want a neck massage? A bedtime story? A bullet in the ear?"

"The latter," she sighed. "And on top of everything else, Mom would be super-pissed that I was seeing you and not trying to leap into your pants."

They both shuddered in unison. They had been friends since the second grade. To Fred, screwing Jonas would have been like screwing a brother. And Jonas liked blonde humans, not blue-haired mermaids.

"And I thought I had a bad day."

"You probably did." Jonas was a chemical engineer for the Aveda corporation. He was constantly struggling to invent a shampoo that didn't damage hair. Which was problematic, as by definition, all shampoos did.

"Speaking of work . . ." He set an Aveda bag positively bulging with, she knew, hair care products, on the table. "Honey, those split ends. I love you, but I can hardly bear to look at you. Seriously. Tend to them. Now."

"It's not my fault I'm wet more than I'm dry."

"Anything else go wrong today? Not that anything had to." The waitress set down two appletinis and he gulped at one thirstily. After a moment's thought, he slammed it down and began on the second one. "Actually, it's not picturing your mom, because she is an awesome-looking woman and I've had a crush on her since you brought me home after the fight . . ."

"Stop it," she said, but she was smiling. Jonas had proudly shown off his no-polish manicure on the first day of second grade, and two fourth graders had discovered rather large problems with their own sexual insecurity. Their solution was to take it out on Jonas. Fred, annoyed at being interrupted from her reading, had broken up the fight by tossing one kid into the monkey bars and dumping the other one, head first, into the sandbox.

Nobody had ever laid a finger on Jonas again through elementary, middle, and high school.

"—and there she was, a blonde angel of mercy, tending to my many wounds, and yelling at you because—"

" 'Violence Isn't The Answer,' " they said in unison.

"Right-o. So I don't mind picturing your mom in the buff, but Sam . . . yech."

"Then they do this whole song and dance about how I'm not Sam's biological child."

Jonas slurped again. "Duh."

"What I said."

"I mean, you're a mermaid and Sam can't get himself out of the shallow end."

"I said that."

"Then what?"

"Then I got my ass back to work and met the new water fellow."

"What the hell is a water fellow? You scientists and your jargon."

"It's a marine biologist who travels around the world trying to explain to the bipeds that they're destroying the planet. He learns and teaches at every place and moves on after three months."

"Hey, hey," Jonas protested mildly. "I'm a biped."

A pretty cute one, too, and Fred was mystified that, at the ripe old age of twenty-nine, Jonas hadn't found someone to settle down with. He was tall, blond, lifted weights, had a black belt in aikido, was a brilliant engineer, was kind to children and small animals, and never judged Fred, not even when they'd gone swimming in the ocean a year after they'd met and he saw her tail.

Maybe it was because he was only eight at the time, and children were more open-minded about such things. Maybe it was because Jonas was generally open-minded about everything. Maybe it was because Jonas was—well, Jonas. Regardless, he had never judged her, he'd stuck staunchly by her, and she didn't have a finer, kinder friend on land or sea.

It made her sad that he was alone, and it drove her mother absolutely batshit. Because she couldn't understand why two people who had known each other forever couldn't settle down together. After all, she had married *her* school buddy.

"So, is he a nice guy? This water fellow?"

"He talked about my hair."

"Well, people usually notice that first."

"About how green it was."

"But it's blue."

She sighed and took a gulp of her margarita. "Never mind."

"So, did you order?"

"Yeah, I've got a salad coming."

"Waited for me like one pig waits for another, huh?" The waitress, as if sensing his need, again showed up out of nowhere. The two of them flirted outrageously while Jonas ordered the lobster and Fred tried not to yawn.

"So, what's next today? I mean, it could hardly get worse."

"New intern."

"Don't tell me: loved dolphins as a kid?"

"Still is a kid. Perky. Cheerful. Gorgeous. Enthusiastic."

"How awful for you." Jonas managed to say such a silly thing with convincing sincerity. "Well, cheer up. She'll only be around for the semester, right? That's how long any of the interns stay."

"Six months is a long goddamned time to put up with Madison Fehr."

"That's her name?"

"And she used to cheer."

"My God! I can't believe you didn't slit your wrists on the way over. What else?"

"I freaked out in the tank again."

"Swam upside down in your scuba suit?" he asked sympathetically.

"Yeah, among other things. And I forgot the fish food. So I'll wait until the place is empty and go back and feed the little buggers."

"Are they still on hunger strike? The fish?"

"I don't want to talk about it."

"I don't want to hear about it. I want to hear about how hot your mom still is."

"Nope."

"Uh . . . your love life?"

"What love life?"

"Right. I'm in the same boat myself. My trainer ran off with my nutritionist."

"Tessa and Mari were lesbians?"

"Apparently so. Leaving me high and dry. My one chance to have a threesome," he sighed, "and it blew right by me."

"Aw. Don't say blew." Fred's salad came, and she picked at it and tried not to flinch as Jonas tore through his lobster.

"I'm not eating one of your pals, am I?" he asked, butter dripping down his chin.

"No. It just makes me slightly ill to watch you devour—"

"A fellow sea citizen?"

"Something I'm allergic to."

Jonas snickered. "A mermaid allergic to shellfish."

"Shut up."

"Come on. It's kind of hilarious. I mean, if you lived in the sea, what the hell would you eat? Would you starve? Or would you slip onto shore, steal food, and race back to the water like the Loch Ness Monster, while people took fuzzy pictures of your bare ass? The only time you ever get sick—you have to admit it's funny."

"I'd like to get through the rest of this day without talking or thinking about bare asses, please."

"So this water fellow guy, what's his name?"

"Thomas Pearson."

"Well, other than needing to change his contact lenses, he seems okay. I mean, you've hardly bitched about him at all. And honey, you bitch about *everything*."

"He's all right. His hair is cute."

Jonas froze, his lobster fork halfway to his mouth. "Oh my God, you're in love."

"I'm not in love."

" 'His hair is cute'? You never say anything nice about anyone. Coming from you, 'cute hair' is a mating call."

"I talked to the guy for thirty seconds. And then he waved at me while I was in the tank."

"Holy fuck, you're getting married, aren't you!"

"Will you simmer? I certainly am not."

Jonas tore through a claw, dunked the meat in butter, and slurped it like spaghetti. "You two were destined to be together. A marine biologist and a marine biologist. Meeting at an aquarium! What are the chances? It's, like, fate. God, what do they put in this butter—nectar?"

Fred pushed her salad away and pointed to his bread. "You going to eat that?"

"And fill up on empty carbs? Go on, take it. You'll swim it off anyway, you rotten bitch."

She grinned and grabbed the bread.

Seven

Fred crept back to the tank a little after midnight, let herself in by one of the employee entrances, climbed the stairs to the top level of Main One, stripped, grabbed a bundle of smelt, and dove in. She shifted from legs to tail without conscious thought; it was like breathing.

And in her mermaid form, it was a lot easier to hear the fish, demanding buggers that they were.

A barracuda passed by. *More fish more fish girl with fish more fish.*

I'm here, aren't I?

A sea turtle floated above. *Pounding more pounding outside pounding.*

Like hell. I'm not playing Pet Shop Boys for you guys anymore and that's it.

As happened with sea creatures confined to the same space for long enough, the fish and turtles and eels and everything else in the tank reverted to a group-mind.

It was nearly deafening.

Not eat not eat NOT EAT!

You'll eat.

NOT EAT NOT EAT NOT EAT!

Shut UP. You think I've got nothing better to do than come here at midnight and wave chum at you? You'll eat what I give you and never mind what I play on the speakers. You can barely hear it in here, anyway.

With the exception of the barracuda and a single shark, the rest of the occupants ignored her fish offerings. And the pair of hunger strike scabs were so loudly shouted down, they swam behind a boulder to sulk together.

Fred knew the hunger strike meant trouble. If they didn't eat, soon the larger fish wouldn't be able to help themselves: they'd prey on the angelfish and sunnies and other small fish stuck in the tank with them. Which would raise questions. Which would get Fred into a lot of trouble with Dr. Barb.

She had to admit she admired their principled stance—especially the smaller fish, who had the most to lose. But like hundreds of little finned "Ghandis" moving in glimmering schools, they valued their dignity (or at least their musical taste) more highly than their own lives.

Morons.

Not to mention the larger problem: she freaking hated the Pet Shop Boys. Any band who relied more on a mixing board than actual talent wasn't, in her mind, a real band. And who was in charge here, anyway?

A damselfish wiggled by. *Pounding more pounding outside pounding.*

Fine! Starve! She dumped the rest of the smelt into the water and lifted herself out of the tank, shaking out her tail and cursing under her breath.

Eight

ॐ

"You have a lot of food left this week," Dr. Barb told her.

"The fish don't seem to be hungry," Fred lied.

"Yeah, and like, that's not Dr. Bimm's problem, right?" Madison chirped, carefully applying lip gloss. "She can't, like, make them eat, right?"

"Umm. That's . . . hmm."

Fred almost grinned at Dr. Barb's discomfiture. She'd since heard through the office grapevine that Madison's parents were descendants of *Mayflower* embarkees (the original tourists and, later, the original illegal immigrants), owned half of the Boston waterfront, and thought their little girl should be able to intern wherever she wished, as long as she wished. And given how dependent the NEA was on private donations . . . "Thank you, Madison. Dr. Bimm, how are the levels?"

"They're perfect." Fred tried not to sound insulted.

"Maybe they don't like the new guy," Thomas joked. He glanced at Madison. "Or girl."

Dr. Barb looked at him over the tops of her reading glasses. "Very funny, Dr. Pearson. I don't like where this is going. If an aquarium guest sees a shark gobble a few angelfish—"

"Stampede?" Thomas guessed.

"And rilly rilly gross, too!"

"Visitors don't want to see blood," Fred said gloomily.

"None of that 'nature, red in tooth and claw' stuff for them, eh?"

"Quite right," Dr. Barb said, handing back Fred's

clipboard. "Keep an eye on it, Dr. Bimm. Let me know if things don't change in the next few days."

"I'm off tomorrow," she reminded her boss.

"Right, right. Well, see how it goes Monday, then."

"Yeah."

"Dr. Pearson, you had something else for us?"

"Well. Yeah."

Fred waited. Dr. Barb waited. Madison blotted her lip gloss. Finally, with poorly concealed impatience, Fred said, "Well?"

"It's just, the levels in the harbor are really off. I mean, by about a thousand percent. And since we're right on the harbor . . ."

"Is that why you were sent here?"

"It's why I came here. I've been sort of following the toxic levels. The source is here, in Boston."

"Oh."

Fred thought for a moment. She hardly ever went into the ocean, vastly preferring Main One or her parents' pool. But she hadn't sensed anything off in the water the last few times she'd jumped in.

On the other hand, she had a ridiculous metabolism. She never got sick. Either mermaids could filter out toxins, or as a hybrid, she wasn't affected by poison in the water.

That's not to say the algae weren't, which would lead to the fish, which would lead to the bipeds.

Not that they cared, exactly.

"I could really use some help figuring this out," Thomas was saying.

"Well, we have several dozen—"

"I was thinking of Dr. Bimm."

"Me?" Fred nearly gasped, badly startled.

"Her?" Madison said, a little sharply. Obviously two coats of lip gloss and sparkly eye shadow had left Pearson unmoved. Certainly he hadn't done more than glance in her direction all morning. Fred wasn't sure why, but she thought that was just fine.

But this?

She was dealing with her parents adopting, a fish strike, trying to find the right woman for Jonas, and still, after twenty-six years, learning to swim. She had no time to play Nancy Drew. "Uh, that's not really my field, Dr. Pearson. I'm just in charge of the big fishie tank." At Dr. Barb's frown, she added, "Main One."

"I could help you, Dr. Pearson!"

Pearson ignored Madison, who had begun to bounce again.

"Oh, come on. I looked you up. You've got just as much book learning as me."

Fred gaped. "Book learning?"

"And I could really use the help," he coaxed, twinkling at her with those amazing dark eyes yet again.

"Yeah, but—"

"And we'd make a great team."

"But—"

"It's settled, then," Dr. Barb commanded.

"What is?" Fred felt like the planet had started spinning faster.

"I could help both of you," Madison announced. Just then, Fred's cell phone trilled the Harry Potter theme.

Saved by the bell. She flipped it open and practically barked, "Yes?"

"Fred, dear, it's Mom."

It was? Her mom sounded rattled. Really rattled. Missing her yoga class three times in a row rattled.

"What's wrong?"

"There's, uh, we have a visitor."

"Okay."

"And he wants to see you."

"Okay."

"Very badly."

"Okay."

"*Very* badly."

Fred puzzled it out. Her mom hadn't been this upset when Fred had caught her on all fours. Who could be visiting? A Republican? After Sam had run the last one off with an empty shotgun, you'd think they would have—

"Well, I'm at work now, but—"

"Yes, I know, but I think you should come home *right now*."

Fred lowered her voice. "Mom, are you in danger?"

"I don't . . . think so."

"Is this stranger standing right there?"

"Yes."

"Put him on."

"I don't think—"

"Mom. Right now."

There was a short silence, and then a deep, gravelly voice said, "Yes?"

"Chum." It wasn't an affectionate nickname. She meant it literally: the fish guts and heads you feed sharks with. "You're scaring the shit out of my mom. Cut it out, unless you want to find out what your colon looks like."

"Fredrika, darling. So nice to hear from you after all this time. Your mother is a charming hostess, but I really insist on speaking with you."

"Oh, we'll speak, chum. You've got my word on that one. But if I get there and she's still freaking out—if she's got so much as a hair out of place—you and I will talk for about thirty days. And you won't like it. At all."

"Looking forward to it," the deep voice purred, and then there was a click.

"Gotta go," Fred said, dropping the clipboard on her desk with a clank and grabbing her purse.

"But—" Dr. Barb and Thomas butted at the same time.

"It's rilly rilly important," she said, and walked out.

Nine

🦭

She didn't bother with the front door. Went around the back, by the kitchen entrance (where her mother's phone was, and where she entertained, and where she was the most comfortable), and kicked in the glass door.

Everyone at the table—Sam, her mother, and the redheaded stranger—froze, then looked up at her. Fred brushed glass out of her hair and stepped into the room.

Dead silence.

"I'm here," she said unnecessarily. Damn. How had glass gotten into her jeans? She wriggled for a second and said, "On your feet, Red. Let's go outside and dance."

"Dance?" the redheaded stranger said blankly. He was looking at her with the oddest expression: admiration, and annoyance, and a little awe.

"Dance. Fight. Smackdown. I'll beat the shit out of you, and you'll go away. Then I'll go back to work before my parents—never mind. Step up. Right now."

"Fred, it's not exactly what you—" Sam began.

"I was a little startled at first," her mom added.

"I apologize if I upset your family," the stranger rumbled. "That was not my intent." He stood up. And up. And up. He towered over all of them, even Fred. *Towered*. He had shoulder-length hair the color of crushed rubies, and eyes that were—okay, were those contacts?—about two shades lighter than his hair. Cherry cough drop–colored eyes.

His shoulders were so broad, she wondered how he'd gotten through the front door. He was dressed in a white shirt, open at the throat, and khaki shorts that showcased his powerfully muscled legs. No shoes, or socks. Big feet. A closely cropped beard the color of his hair. A broad forehead, a strong chin. And that voice! Deep, rumbling . . . like verbal velvet.

"But I think it's fine to step outside."

"What?"

"I think it's fine to step outside," the stranger repeated. "Or we could make use of your sire's pond."

"My what's what?"

"The pool." In a low voice, as if Fred couldn't hear perfectly well, he bent down (and down, and down) and murmured into her mom's ear, "Is something wrong with her mind?"

"No," her mom practically snapped. "She's a Ph.D., for crying out loud. Don't do that, it's freaky."

"Get away from her," Fred ordered, still edgy. Okay, she was usually edgy. But it had been a rough forty-eight hours.

"It's all right, Fred. I'm sorry I scared you. It's just—you're not the only one who makes dramatic entrances. This is—well—this is the High Prince Artur."

"Prince Artur," Fred repeated, like a parrot.

"Of the Black Sea," the stranger added helpfully.

"He says—he says you're one of his subjects," her mom continued.

"Oh, does he?"

"And that you owe him fealty and loyalty and such."

"Really."

The prince bowed. "It is always my great pleasure to meet a comely new subject."

"Really."

"And we, uh, we didn't really know what to think when he showed up and said all this and also said— uh—"

"Spit it, Mom."

"That your father is dead," her mom said, and burst into tears.

"Good lady," the prince said, looking distressed for the first time, "I did not mean to upset you so. I had been told you but barely knew each other and that my subject had known your mate as her sire."

"We only spent an hour together but—but now Fred will never meet him. And I'll never get to thank him for giving her to me." Her mother covered her eyes like a child and sobbed.

"Okay, that's *it*. Get away from her right now."

The prince ignored her. "Our people will tell her all she wishes to know. And her sire was—he was not the type to appreciate his progeny," the prince said carefully.

"Bio father was kind of a dick, huh?" Fred guessed.

The prince patted her mother, almost sending her sprawling, then straightened. "Shall we adjourn?"

"Now? Right now?"

"Yes. Shall we?"

Fred noticed it was a command disguised as a question. But even though they seemed to be getting along, she was wild to get this huge redhead away from her folks. "Okay. Sorry about the door, Mom."

"It was one of your more dramatic entrances," her mom said, perking up right away. "I kind of liked it."

"Indeed," the stranger murmured, and led the way to the pool as if it were his house and not the place she'd grown up.

Ten

🐟

"So. High Prince Artur—can I call you Art?"

"You may not." The prince was—*eep*—stripping. The shirt went flying, followed by the pants. No underwear, she couldn't help but notice. Then he dove into the saltwater pool, giving her a glimpse of a muscular back and taut buttocks, and then he was under.

She squatted by the side of the pool. "Well, I'm sure as hell not calling you Your Highness," she yelled to the water. "I live on land. I'm not one of your damned subjects!"

He popped up, water glistening in his beard, and grinned at her, showing a great many teeth. Almost . . . pointy? How had she not noticed *that* before? "Oh yes you are, Little Rika."

"Fred."

"Ugh."

"Fred. Not Rika. Not Ugh. Fred. Not little anything. I'm five ten, for crying out loud."

"Little Rika," he said, and dove back down, splashing her with his tail.

His tail.

His *tail*?

Much longer than hers, wider at the hips, too. A much darker green than hers. The fins were wider at the base, and longer. She instantly deduced he was a faster, stronger swimmer—and she'd never met anyone or anything, land or sea, that could beat her in the water.

Well, shit.

"So why are you here?" she said to the water.

He popped up again and blew a stream of water at her. She ducked, cursing, and nearly fell in. "Come in and we will talk about it."

"I'm—" *Not getting naked in front of you*, was her first thought, which is when her mom spoke up in her head: *nudity is beautiful and natural*, blah-blah.

It wasn't getting naked. She didn't have much modesty. She always swam in the nude, unless she had to wiggle into that awful scuba suit. It was swimming with a merman. Someone like her. Except not like her: she hadn't inherited the strong, pointy teeth (doubtless for chomping through raw fish and bone), or the more powerful tail. Did she want to invite comparisons?

Fuck him and fuck what he thinks.

She stood, pulled off her shoes and socks, shucked off her jeans and panties, tossed her sweater over her head, unsnapped her bra, and dove over his head, straight down.

He came down at once, staring at her with unashamed curiosity.

You look . . . different.

Of course. Telepathy. How else would mer-people talk under water?

Shut up. Why are you here?

I need you.

Do tell.

He swam closer and reached for her waist; she smacked his hand away, hard.

My subjects do not treat me thus.

Tell someone who gives a ripe shit.

They invite my caresses.

They need drugs. What do you want?

You, of course.

Yes, but for what?

He floated thoughtfully, then zipped past her with a powerful flex of his tail. She turned to watch him go by, and suddenly he was behind her, his arms wrapped around her waist where her scales met flesh. She felt a tingle that shot from her brain straight down her spinal cord and . . . lower.

She tossed an elbow back and caught him in the throat, which accomplished several things: he coughed explosively, sending out a stream of bubbles; let go; swam back and let her get some distance.

Hands off, chum.

You are unlike any of my people, Little Rika. I cannot resist you.

Try hard, chum. And it's Fred. Got it? F-R-E-D. She swam irritably past him, keeping an eye on his hands.

It is unfair that you have an affectionate nickname for me and I am not allowed one for you.

Affectionate . . . ? Oh, hell.

Last time: what do you want? Cough up or I'm back on tile before you can say "ow, my balls!"

My what?

Chum!

All right, Little Rika, do not distress yourself.

You haven't seen me distressed yet.

The bipeds are poisoning the harbor waters.

As far as thunderous announcements went, that one was weak.

She shrugged. *That's what bipeds do.*

My father, the High King, has charged me with finding you and enlisting your help to stop it.

Your father, the High King, can take a long walk off a short—

As one of our subjects, you are thus charged to aid us until our task is finished.

Well, lucky lucky me.

Wait. What had Pearson been babbling about? Toxins in the harbor?

Oh, hell.

Can you walk around on land for a few hours?

I do not like the surface, he admitted, swimming circles around her (literally), *but I can tolerate the environment as long as I must.*

Swell. Because I'm thinking there's someone you should meet.

She shot up to the surface, switched back to legs, and climbed out. She heard Artur come up behind her, but luckily for his continued good health, he didn't try to grab her again.

"Someone like you?" he asked, almost eagerly.

"No," she replied. "Not like me at all."

Eleven

Jonas stopped dead in his tracks when he saw Fred and who she was sitting with.

"Whoa," he said by way of greeting.

"Jonas, Prince Artur of the Black Sea. Art, Jonas."

"Prince what of the *what*? Oh my God! Your hair! Your eyes!" The prince courteously stood and Jonas wrung the man's hand like Fred would wring a wet washcloth, craning his neck to stare up at the man. "Have you thought about modeling?"

"I do not know what that is."

"Didn't you get my message?" Fred bitched. "I told you our dinner thing was cancelled."

"Oh, you always try to punk out on me. I didn't think you had, you know, an actual real reason. Like a date!"

"It's not a date," Fred began, but Jonas was already sliding into the seat beside Fred, forcing her to move over or be squashed.

"Hi, I'm Jonas, like the lady said. So, what's up with you, dude?"

"Bipeds are poisoning our waters."

Jonas arched a blond brow and turned to Fred. "So you were saying the other day. What's going on?"

Fred shrugged. "Nothing new."

"Nothing new? Have you *seen* this guy?" he cried as if Artur wasn't sitting three feet away. "Is he like you? He's a mer-dude, isnt' he?"

"Yeah," she sighed. "A mer-dude."

The waiter stopped by the table, set a tray of sushi in front of Artur and a bowl of miso soup in front of Fred, took Jonas's order and glided away.

"So again with this biped thing?" Jonas demanded. "What are you talking about?"

Artur quietly ate his sushi (with his fingers, she noticed; probably didn't get much practice with chopsticks at the bottom of the ocean) and said nothing. Fred assumed it was up to her to explain.

"Jonas, I *know* the bipeds are wrecking the planet. You—they—can't help it. As far as they're concerned, they don't feel the sea; it's just something else to claim and fish and gut and leave dead."

"Uh," Jonas said. He paused, then, again: "Uh."

"Quite right," Artur agreed with his mouth full.

"Come on," he protested. "We're not that bad."

Both Fred and Artur stared at him stonily.

Jonas, the chemical engineer, couldn't keep up the façade. "Okay, we're pretty bad. We wreck the planet and we're not potty trained. But I don't think anybody's dumping bad stuff in the water to—I mean, on pur—uh . . ." He trailed off, no doubt hearing the absurdity of his words.

Fred sucked down half her miso soup, waited to

see if her tongue would blister, then said, "I still don't know why you want my help. I'll be frank—"

"Not Fred?" Artur teased, tossing a chunk of tuna sushi into his mouth.

"—and tell you I'm not real interested in solving your little mystery. I just wanna feed the fish and stay out of my mom's living room for the rest of my life. Like I said to Dr. Pearson—tried to say—it's not really my field."

"The sea belongs to you, as well."

"Oh, sure. All the mer-guys would welcome me with open arms."

"They would." In went some halibut. "And if they did not, they would answer to me. Would you like some? It's very fresh."

Fred shuddered and slurped more miso. "No."

"Fred's allergic to seafood," Jonas explained.

"You—you are?" Artur's jaw was sagging, which annoyed her to no end. "But—but what do you *eat*?"

"Everything else."

"So, your plan is . . . what?" Jonas was tapping his

fingers on the table in an irritating rhythm. "You're gonna be the Dr. Watson to his Sherlock?"

Fred shuddered; she couldn't help it.

"You don't want to?"

"I don't care."

"So give him the old heave-ho."

"Apparently," she said dryly, "I'm one of his subjects and have to do whatever he wants."

"Since when has *authority* stopped you from being you?"

"Well. How weird is it that in forty-eight hours two guys show up both bitching about the same thing?"

"You're gonna team him up with the water fellow?"

"That's the plan."

"What is a water fellow?"

"Eat your dead fish," she told Artur. To Jonas: "Let them team up and solve the mystery. Let me get back to work. Everybody's happy."

Jonas was holding his head in his hands. Fred

ignored it. Artur looked slightly alarmed. "Good sir, what ails you?"

"Artur, could you give us a minute, please?"

Without a word, Artur rose, crossed the room in four big strides, and started talking to their waitress, who was staring at him the way diabetics stared at sundaes.

"What?"

"Fred, what the hell is wrong with you?"

"What?"

"You've met two new guys and instead of, I dunno, trying to build a meaningful relationship or at least get laid by either or both of them, you're gonna match them up together and head back to the aquarium?"

"Yeah."

"Fred. You are dumber than an octopus."

"Octopi," she told him with raised eyebrows, "are among the smartest animals on earth."

"Why don't you guys work together? Huh? He came all the way from the Black Sea—where the hell *is* the Black Sea, anyway . . . well, it sounds far away—and you can't just dump him!"

"I can." She added, "Southeastern Europe. Oh, and Asia Minor."

"What?"

"The Black Sea. Connected to the Mediterranean by the Bosphorus and the Sea of Marmara, and to the Sea of Azov by the—"

"This is not the point—"

"—Strait of Kerch," she finished.

She ignored his moan of despair and fished the last piece of tofu out of her soup bowl. The fact was, both Thomas and Artur made her anxious. She wasn't used to attention from men. And she had no interest in being in a triangle. Not that *that* was likely to happen.

"When was the last time you went on a date?" Jonas was demanding. "And if you give me the patented Fred 'I don't give a shit' shrug, I'll beat you to death."

She laughed at him. Then thought about it. And thought. And thought some more. "Dr. Barb's ex-husband," she said at last.

"Oh, God, that's right. I totally forgot about him. You're lucky you didn't lose your job over that one."

"She's the one who set us up," Fred reminded him. What neither of them needed reminding of was that it was a complete disaster. Dr. Barb's ex, whose name Fred had by now forgotten, spent half the date making gross passes at Fred, and the other half pining for his ex-wife. They had ended the meeting with a handshake, and he'd gone home with a black eye when he'd tried too persistently for more.

"And ever since then, you've been stuck in the vortex of a—what? Six? Six-year dating dry spell?"

"Vortex?"

"And here's two hunky fellows climbing all over you—"

"They aren't—"

"—and all you can think of to do is stick them together and vamoose."

"I've got other stuff to worry about."

"That's why," he said kindly, "you're a moron. Just like an octopus. No, don't tell me, I don't care. They're stupid, too."

Twelve

 ʒ

Jonas cheerfully trailed behind his best bud and her massive, ridiculously good-looking new pal. He eyed the people milling around on the cobblestones and wondered if any of them had the faintest idea he was walking behind two mer-people. Hell, *he* had a hard time believing it, and he'd grown up with one of them.

Artur kept leaning over and trying to whisper in Fred's ear, and she kept batting him away like he was a persistently annoying fly. Jonas shook his head. It was so obvious that Artur—a prince! A freakin' prince!—had the hots for his pal. Did she notice? Nuh-uh. Would she have cared if she did notice? Probably not. Was she a nutjob of the highest order? Yup.

But then, if she didn't engage in that odd Freddish behavior, she wouldn't be Fred.

He still remembered the day they met. He'd been pretty shocked when the big kids had ganged up on him, and had barely noticed the small, stick-thin, blue-haired girl reading a book up against a tree.

Whether she didn't like the distraction from her book or couldn't stand to see the odds so badly out of whack (probably the former), it didn't matter. She'd gotten up and put her hands on the big kids and they'd gone flying, and then she went back to her book and ignored the stares and the whispers. Almost as if, at the ripe old age of seven, she didn't notice them anymore, or never had, or just didn't care.

He'd pestered her the rest of the day until she had sighed and agreed to bring him to her house. They'd been buds ever since.

He'd known. Not that she was a mermaid, but

even as a child, Fred wasn't like anybody else. *Anybody* else. That was all right, though, because he wasn't a typical elementary school student, either, not when he knew how to do floral arrangements and had a collection of paint chips that he kept organized by tint and type (matte, gloss, et cetera).

And when she'd finally worked up the courage to show him her other form, he had been surprised, but not shocked. And not horrified, either. He'd thought her tail was pretty, and had told her so. She'd told him to shut up, and he'd ignored her.

Now he was tagging along, as he so often did, partly because he smelled excitement, and partly because he was hoping to get another glimpse of the delectable Dr. Barb. He'd been wondering for years what her hair would feel like in his hands—if it ever was out of that silly braid—if her eyes narrowed or widened or closed completely during orgasm. It was a full-on crush, the one secret he kept from Fred. Just the thought of her scorn (or indifference) made him cringe.

"It's pretty late," Fred said over her shoulder, leading them to a darkened employee entrance. "I doubt anybody's around. Which is good. Technically neither of you should be here."

"Technically, you're a frigid bitch," he reminded her.

"Shut up."

"*You* shut up."

Fred sighed. "Are you ever going to leave the second grade?"

"Are you ever going to do anything about those split ends?"

She ignored him, the way she ignored the stare Artur gave her. That was also business as usual. He'd long given up trying to point out the guys (and occasional gal) checking her out pretty much daily.

Fred wasn't gorgeous, but she had—something. The hair, of course. The long legs and waist. Skinny, so she could wear anything and look good. And the height. He had barely an inch on her. Altogether, she was a striking, if startling, woman.

And the smile. Fred had a perfectly beautiful smile,

he happened to know from seeing it three, maybe four times in twenty years.

And a wonderful sense of humor. The trouble was . . .

He thought about it. The trouble was, she was also the loneliest person he knew. And it wasn't hard to figure why. She worked so hard shoving people away, nobody had a chance to dump her first. Psych 101, plain and simple.

"Yeah," he replied, "but Dr. Barb doesn't have a life any more than you do."

"Says the moron tagging along at ten thirty at night on a Friday." She turned, walked backward for a second, and narrowed her sea green eyes. "What do you care if Dr. Barb is here?"

"I'm just warning you," he covered.

"Muh," she replied, turning back around.

And lo and behold, the gods of frustrated sexual yearnings smiled on him as the employee door slammed open and out darted Dr. Barb! Who, he happened to know, trotted everywhere, like a little kid. She nearly slammed into Fred, checked herself, skidded to a halt, straightened, blew her bangs out of her eyes, and said, "Dr. Bimm! You're back. Everything all right at home, I trust?"

Instantly, Jonas seized Artur and dragged him away so Dr. Barb wouldn't realize Fred had been about to sneak two unauthorized persons into the NEA in the middle of the night. There was a convenient corner near the outdoor seal tank and he hissed, "Put your arms around me."

"Pardon?"

"Like we're boyfriends."

"No."

"Look," he snapped, "I don't like it any more than you do, but d'you want Fred to get into trouble?"

Stiffly, like a recently animated marble statue, Artur placed his arms around Jonas's waist.

"Not like *that*. You look like someone's sticking a gun in your ear."

"Someone will most likely have to very soon."

"Put some feeling in it," he commanded. "Love me tender!"

"No."

"Look, I'd much rather be snuggling with *her*." He jerked a thumb over his shoulder. "But we can't get caught, okay? And we can't get Fred into trouble. So snuggle. Now."

Instead of snuggling, Artur grabbed him by the shirtfront and hoisted him to eye level. This was the most alarming thing to happen since he had tried to invent chocolate shampoo and had blown up Lab Six.

"You do not touch her," Artur was telling him, while Jonas struggled and kicked, his feet a good foot off the ground. "Ever. Do you understand, biped?"

"Not—one of—your subjects," he coughed.

"Then I will simply have to beat you until you comply."

"This shirt—cost—one-fifty—at Macy's—" he gurgled.

Artur set him down (reluctantly, it seemed to Jonas).

"Good thing you did that," he said, straightening his clothing and blowing his hair out of his eyes, "because I was about to kick your fishy ass into the seal tank."

Artur laughed politely.

"Crushin' on Fred, eh?" It had to be Fred. It sure as shit better not be Dr. Barb or there'd be a beat-down, all right, and Mr. Hotshit Prince might get a surprise.

"I do not know what that—"

"Yes you do. Get in line, pal. But don't worry about me. Fred and I are nothing more than friends. Just realize there are other men out there. Even if . . ."

"Even if . . . ?"

"She's oblivious."

Artur nodded, stroking his too-cool red beard. Not too long, not absurdly short—like the little bear in Goldilocks, it was just right. "That is well," he said at last.

"Oh, right, real well. Listen—"

"Morons!" Fred's grating voice cut through their private chat. "Are you coming, or not?"

"Where's Dr. Barb?" he asked, peeking around the corner to make sure the coast was clear.

"She's outta here. Didn't even notice you."

"Oh," Jonas said. He faked enthusiasm. "That's good, then."

Fred gave him an odd look, and let them into the darkened halls of the NEA.

Thirteen

"It should be here somewhere."

"What exactly are we looking for, Nancy Drew?"

Fred gave Jonas a look. They'd both gone through an insane Drew phase in the fourth grade, read the entire Nancy Drew series, talked about her and her friends and her borderline-absentee dad, and at the end had both decided it was a miracle Ms. Drew lived through any of her wacky adventures.

"What. Are. We. Looking. For?"

"I heard you the first time, moron. Anything

Dr. Pearson might have left. He's got to have notes, charts—something."

"I dislike this skulking about," the prince said, looking around the small, cluttered lab with distaste. "It ill becomes royalty. I prefer action."

"Indulge the commoners, will ya?"

"Yeah, do that." Fred picked up a clipboard and instantly became absorbed. Much more interesting than listening to the men in her life bitch and moan. How did wives and moms stand it?

"I don't know why I'm here," Jonas was saying, looking absently around the lab. "It's not really my field. Now, if you want to talk about a hand cream that doubles as perfume . . ."

"I don't know why you're here either." Jonas, she had decided three years ago, had an odd affection for the NEA. He'd been in it about a thousand times, and was always chatting up her boss and colleagues . . . even the volunteers who worked the gift shop. She happened to know he didn't give a tin shit about oceans, sea life, stuffed seals or penguins, so it was a bit of a mystery. "So go."

"Yeah, maybe I will." In another of his odd mood swings, Jonas had gone from keen interest to yawning boredom in less than thirty.

"Then be off," the prince commanded, sitting on a lab stool and nearly toppling off when he realized the chair didn't have a back.

Fred swallowed a laugh and kept her gaze glued to the clipboard. Pearson had the handwriting of a serial killer, and she was having a tough time deciphering if this was a toxin sheet or his grocery list.

"You're pretty strong," she heard Jonas say to Artur, obviously ignoring the prince's command to "be off." "Fred is, too. I once saw her pick up her mom's fridge to get one of my Hot Wheels."

"That is interesting about Fred. It is also an accurate observation."

"I'm guessing it's the whole mer-angle, right? I mean, you can't swim around on the bottom of the ocean day and night—all that pressure—and not build some upper body strength. I mean, you guys are under *literal* pressure, not the usual 'the HR rep hates me, I can't stand office politics' pressure."

"Do not feel shame. An air breather is by nature much weaker."

"Uh—okay, yeah, I'm not really a shame-feelin' kinda guy, but thanks anyway. I'm betting you can see in the dark like a cat, too, huh?"

"What is a cat?"

"Because I bet it gets pretty dark down there, too, right?"

"It is dark in many places," the prince said, sounding slightly confused. She couldn't blame him. Jonas had all the tact of a pit bull once his mind starting chewing on a problem.

"So all mer-people—"

"Undersea Folk," the prince corrected.

Fred resisted the urge to roll her eyes. Well, he could have picked a worse one, like Ben-Varry or Caesg or Meerfrau. Seemed like all of her research on mer-folk came up with stuff that was ninety percent outright wrong, and silly-sounding names.

"Right, right, that's what I meant. All Undersea Folk are super strong, and can see in the dark, and can breathe air and water—how *do* you breathe air and water?"

"We just—do." Artur looked from Fred to Jonas, puzzled. "Are you not comrades? How do you not know these things about a friend?"

"Because *Fred* doesn't know a lot of these things. She was raised by humans. Heck, I didn't even know she was a fellow mammal at first, because she's so clammy all the time. You think her mom ever let her near a doctor?"

"I'm never sick," Fred said absently.

"Anyway, back to what we were talking about. Fred doesn't have gills. Not even when she has a tail."

"Never mind her tail," the prince ordered. "And why would she? She is not part fish. She is one of the Undersea Folk. She is one of *my* people."

"Oh, take a pill, handsome. I'm just making observations, here, and you're getting all touchy." He added, oddly, "Resist the urge to pick me up and shake me like a juice box."

Artur sighed, the quiet groan of a man picking up a heavy, chattering burden. "We pull air into our bodies when we are on land, and when we are under water we pull air from the water."

"Okay, that was super helpful. Lemme just grab some clarification, 'kay? So—like, you get oxygen from the water, how? The cells of your body somehow open up and grab the oxygen and bring it into your system? You're, what, like starfish?"

Close, Fred thought. It really was difficult to explain. Just as people didn't think about breathing, she didn't think about water-breathing.

No, she didn't have gills, and she wasn't half girl, half fish, but a mammal that simply resembled such a creature. A large, hostile mammal whose baseline temp was eighty-eight degrees and whose resting heart rate was thirty.

She just—just never needed to come up for air when she was swimming. Interesting that even though she had a doctorate in marine biology she never gave much thought to her *own* biology. (Though it had been amusing, picturing her professors' reactions if she had shown off her tail during a wet lab.) Very likely the pores in her skin were able to extract oxygen from the—

"This is useless," she said, bored with the "how do you not drown" talk, and annoyed with Pearson's notes. "A bad idea. We should have come during business hours."

"Oh, sure," Jonas said snarkily. "*That* would have been easy to explain. 'Hi, Dr. Barb, this is the Prince of the—' "

Fred gave him a look. "Don't you have somewhere to be?"

"Sobbingly, no."

"Well, let's think about this. I'd like to try feeding the fish again, anyway, so I might as well do it while we're here. You—what's your plan?"

"For what?" Artur replied, looking startled when she pointed at him.

"For—you know. Waiting until tomorrow to meet the *other* guy who's bugging me about your little problem."

"I will return with you to your dwelling, of course."

"What?" she cried. "I don't have the room or the temperament for a royal roommate. And don't wait for an invitation or anything."

"You are my subject," he said, looking even more wide-eyed. "Of course you will open your home to me."

Jonas snickered. "Fred, meet Artur. Artur, meet Fred."

"I do not know what you—"

"Fred doesn't 'of course' do anything."

"There's a Marriott right next door," she forced through a tense jaw. "We'll get you a room. You might be in town for a while."

"The Prince of the Black Sea has an American Express?" Jonas asked gleefully, being more annoying than usual. Then, before Artur could ask what he was talking about: "You got any money on you? Dough? Moolah? Treasure?"

Artur's red eyes actually glowed with comprehension. "Ah! Treasure. Yes, of course. The sea is generous. But I—"

"No pockets, huh? Left all your doubloons at home?"

"Yes."

"I'll put the room on my Visa," Fred gritted.

"You refuse your home to me?"

"Yes."

"You may not."

"It's a one-bedroom apartment. Just watch me."

Artur glared at her. She glared back. Jonas watched, enjoying himself far too much. Then they both glared at him.

"Well, I'm sure you two will work it out." He coughed. "I'll just, you know, hit the trail. Call me tomorrow," he said to Fred.

"Nuh," she said, fumbling through the papers on Pearson's desk. The guy had been in town less than three days and his lab looked like a tsunami had hit it. How he could find anything, much less research his little problem, was beyond her. "This is hopeless. My dumb idea of the year. I'd better see to the fish." She thought of something and looked up at Artur, who was still looking at her with narrowed eyes. "You any good with fish? I mean, do they listen to you?"

"Of course."

She sighed. "Of course."

"Of course," Jonas called over his shoulder as he left.

"Well, suit up. Or whatever you do."

"Summon an underling to tend to your chore," he said, waving her responsibilities away with a hand the size of a baseball glove. "Greater problems require your attention."

"Around here, *I'm* the underling," she snapped. "Some of us work for a living, Prince Artur."

He blinked, his eyes like banked coals in the poor light of the lab. Creepy eyes. But kind of interesting. Hard to look away from, really. "I can assure you, setting out from the Black Sea to find you was considerable work."

"Good for you. Let's go."

"Where?"

"More subjects for you to meet."

Fourteen

🐚

"Those tiny creatures are not my subjects," the prince observed, staring down into Main One. They were at the top level of the aquarium, the observation deck, looking down into the main tank. The prince, on the way up, pronounced the NEA "acceptable," deciding it was "a miniature kingdom." She had bitten back an acid remark; maybe he'd decide to take the place over and give her a new problem to worry about.

"But they'll listen to you, right?"

"Some will. The predators will."

"And the others?"

He smiled at her with his very sharp teeth. "The others will see me as the predator, and flee."

Briefly, she imagined herself explaining the mass carnage to Dr. Barb. "Ohhh . . . kay. New plan. How about you stay here, then? I'll do this myself."

He eyed the smelt bucket with distaste. "These menial tasks are beneath you."

She cursed herself for not having Jonas take Artur with him when he left. Jonas could have checked him into the Marriott, gotten the guy all settled, fluffed his pillows, told him all about the good bars, whatever. Now *she* was stuck with him. "Why?"

"Because—" He groped. Not literally, thank God. "Because you are above such things."

She prayed the Marriott still had rooms at this hour. "Why?"

"Because you should be tended to and coddled and pleasured and teased."

She gaped at him. He was staring down at her, his big hands in his pockets, his eyes thoughtful and almost—dreamy? "Why?"

"Would you like to be a princess, Little Rika? I think that would suit you. I think that would suit you very well."

"Artur, do you have to take any medications if you're out of the water for a while?" She racked her brain, trying to figure out the poor guy's damage. "Do you need to lie down, maybe? Do you feel dehydrated? Do you have a headache? I don't think you're getting enough air. Or probably too much air. Yeah, that's it!" In her excitement, she reached out and grabbed his arm. He felt just right; not feverish, like Jonas felt on the few occasions she'd touched him. "Do you feel light-headed? Dizzy?"

Somehow, he had edged closer without her noticing. Now he was *very* close. Almost kissing close. "Yes," he murmured.

"You do? You feel dizzy?"

"Yes."

"When your king father sent you, he didn't warn you? That you might not be able to take it?"

"As a matter of fact, he did not."

"Well," she fretted, "you'd better lie down."

"Yes indeed." His hand was on the back of her neck. He probably didn't want to fall down. Which was too bad, because if he went, they both would. She doubted she could keep him from—

His lips covered hers and pressed, hard. No tentative brushing of lips for *this* guy. No, his mouth was all over hers, almost hard enough to bruise, and his fingers were like iron on her neck, it was overwhelming, it was the hardest, most possessive kiss of her life and she brought her hands up in outraged surprise, tried to shove him away except, weirdly, she wasn't shoving him. She was touching, feeling . . . stroking?

Was *she* getting too little air?

She managed to tear free and leaned on Pearson's desk, gasping. "That's—don't do that."

"Oh, I think I will, Little Rika. It was far better than I imagined, and I have a *large* . . . imagination."

She stared at him, her mouth hanging open, and her brain once again erroneously reported that the planet's spin had sped up. It was all—it was just too much.

It was *too much*, really! For anyone to deal with. Her mom on all fours. Her dad not being her dad.

Her dad being *dead*. Pearson showing up. This one showing up. Somebody poisoning the harbor. This one sticking around. Pearson waving at her—following her all the way down the tank to wave at her. This one all grabby. Pearson all chatty about her hair. This one—

"Are you well, Little Rika?"

"No."

"I did not think so. You look odd."

"I have to go to work," she said, feeling stupid. That wasn't what she had meant to say. At all. Why couldn't she think of what she meant?

He shrugged, turned his back, dismissed her, started heading down the stairs. "Then work. I will view the displays, like a good biped termist."

"Tourist."

"That, yes."

"Don't eat any of the exhibits," she couldn't help adding, then fled.

Fifteen

She hopped on one foot, struggling out of her stubborn shoe, and it seemed as if everything was fighting her: items of clothing, the doorknob, the packets of smelt. Breathless, she hit the water and grew a tail.

Fish girl bring fish.

And realized she was still gasping from the kiss. Jonas's inquisitive comments about how mermaids breathed without gills—

Fish girl bang bang fish girl bang.

—flitted past her brain and she realized her mouth was closed. So she was gasping in her brain.

Fish girl bring bang bang thud thud.

Or thought she was gasping.

Fish girl bring bang bang thud thud.

Or—

Fish girl bring BANG BANG THUD THUD.
EVERYBODY SHUT THE HELL UP!

Startled, an angelfish swam into a chunk of coral reef, reeled dizzily for a foot, then straightened and darted away.

She took a deep breath. Or thought she did. And tried to think. Yes, get Artur into the Marriott Long Wharf tonight, *tonight*, then get

(sneak)

the hell back to her apartment on Commonwealth Avenue. Tomorrow was another day, and all that. Yes.

How she would keep a strong-willed, large, immensely powerful man at arm's length was tomorrow's problem. She just—didn't he understand? This wasn't how things were supposed to be.

She offered fish to fish, and some of them, cowed

from her mental screeching, actually fed. Distractedly, she fed several reef fish and a couple of the turtles. The sharks grinned as they swam by, and ignored her offerings. That was all right, though. She had plenty of other problems right now. So many that she couldn't be elated that some of the fish had given in without her having to blast "West End Girls" over the PA system.

For example, the tourists and what they'd think if the sharks turned on, say, the eels at exactly the wrong moment. Like the guy she could see through the window. He'd probably freak out at a feeding frenzy. Or maybe he'd get off on it; you never could tell. A bigger problem was that the guy was here wicked late—the place had closed a couple hours ago. Did they even *have* security guards in this place anymore?

And what *was* he doing? Leaning on one of the fifty-two windows and staring at her. Like there weren't 650 other fish in the tank to glare at. No, he had to gawk at her. When were the tourists going back to wherever the hell they spawned? Wasn't it autumn already?

Well? *Wasn't it?*

She irritably tossed another smelt and glowered at the dark-haired gawker, then realized with something like relief that it wasn't a tourist, it was Thomas Pearson. Hmm, another geek with no life; he'd fit right in at NEA. Why else would he come back to the aquarium in the wee hours of a Friday night?

And he was looking right at her. Guess he was giving the toxins a rest. Was that flattering or annoying?

You have a tail right now.

She had a tail right now. She'd been so distracted from Artur's top tank pawing that she'd completely—

Their eyes met across a crowded tank of fish. Thomas's face was actually squashed up against the glass, "the better to see you with, my dear." His hands were plastered flat. His breath fogged the pane.

Then he vanished.

She dropped the smelt, put her arms over her head, and with a powerful flick of her tail shot to the top of the tank. She thought, *Right this minute he's sprinting up the stairs. That's three flights he's got to go up. I can—*

What? Haul her big white butt out of the tank, dry

off, get into her clothes, and pretend it was some *other* green-haired mermaid in the NEA tank?

She grabbed the edge of the tank and flicked her tail, just as Thomas galloped into the observation room. He was breathing hard and his dark hair had tumbled into his eyes. He jerked his bangs back and clutched his collar, actually yanked at it until the top button flew off and exposed his throat. He gulped air and she thought, *Good thing he wasn't wearing a tie or he might have been strangled.*

He pointed at her, his big dark eyes practically bulging from his head. "I knew it!" he practically screamed. "I knew you weren't like all the others!"

"Dr. Pearson," she began, but trailed off in mystification as he ran to her, lost his balance, actually slid on his knees until he was leaning against the top of the tank, and then leaned over and kissed her spang on the mouth.

Okay. I guess it's just going to be that kind of a day. The kind where men I've just met have this odd illness where they can't keep their hands off me.

"Dr. Pearson," she tried again, but "ffgggrrrll" is

what came out, since he was still kissing her. And she was kissing him back, holding on to his shirt so she wouldn't drop the rest of the way back into the tank. His lips were warm, almost hot; they were burning her, he was *scorching* her with his kisses, and she wasn't minding. No, she wasn't minding at all.

His hands on her shoulders were equally hot, making her think about rolling around under the sheets with him on a cold winter day, when the only way to stay warm was to snuggle with the guy in the bed with—

Weirdly, he was gone. Like he had teleported. Or been grabbed from behind and hauled away from her. But Pearson was a big guy. Who'd be strong enough to—

"Artur, don't!"

She almost covered her eyes; it was going to be too awful. Pearson, looking astonished. Artur, red eyes slits of rage. Pearson, looking not exactly happy himself. She opened her mouth to yell—what? She had no idea.

Then Thomas whipped an elbow back, catching

Artur in the throat. This loosened the giant redhead's grip long enough for Fred to realize that Pearson was going to—yep, she knew that move from watching Jonas's self-defense tournaments. Thomas grabbed Artur's left arm and threw the guy over his shoulder, right into Main One.

Artur hit with a spectacular splash, wriggled around beneath the surface for a moment, and then popped up beside Fred, his shorts whirling toward the bottom of the tank, momentarily covering a sea turtle. Artur's tail was easily seen in the water—more easily, in fact, than Fred's had been.

Thomas gaped down at them. They stared up.

"Okay," Thomas said after a long moment. "I'm gonna need a minute here." And he sat down on the deck, propped his exhausted chin in his hands and just gawked at them both.

Sixteen

🦐

"Until you came along, nobody but Jonas knew my secret," Fred bitched.

"Do not keep your rightful self hidden."

"Who's to say legs aren't my rightful self? I'm just as much a human as I am a mermaid."

"Undersea Folk."

"Don't correct me! If I want to call myself a Havmand there's not a damned thing you can do about it."

"Havmand?"

"Scandinavian mermaid," Thomas called, still staring at them like a kid getting his Saturday morning cartoon fix.

"Right. Or a—wait." She focused on Thomas who, she was relieved to see, no longer looked like he was going to stroke out. "Oh, don't tell me."

He shrugged. "I'm afraid so."

"What?" Artur asked sharply.

"Mermaid geek," Fred sighed. There were, she had noticed as a grad student, three types who went for the doctorate in marine biology: women who *lurrrved* dolphins as little girls (see: Madison, the annoying); men and women who wanted to come up with the newest bioactive drug and make big bucks working at a pharmaceutical company (see: the greedy); and men who fantasized about mermaids. Thomas, it appeared, had no interest in pharmacology or dolphins.

"I am not surprised at all," Thomas was saying. "That's what's so surprising."

"Sure. You staggered around looking like an M.I. about to happen because you were unsurprised."

"M.I.?" Artur asked.

"Heart attack."

"Okay, I was taken off guard for a few moments. But I've since recovered," he insisted, still pale. "Because I've had this theory since I was eight—"

"Yeah. Well. Theory realized."

He crept closer. "So, obviously you're more the Daryl Hannah–type mermaid than the Hans Christian Andersen–type—"

"That's enough of that," she said, nicely enough.

"Is this the biped you wished me to meet?"

"Huh? Oh. Prince Artur, this is Dr. Thomas Pearson. Thomas, this is Artur, High Prince of the Black Sea."

Thomas had scooted all the way up to the edge of the tank as she talked, and now stuck his arm out. Artur leaned up, balancing on his tail like a dolphin, and they shook hands. Thomas nearly fell in while trying not to make it obvious he was still staring at them. "Nice to meet you. Sorry about kicking your ass right into the tank like that. You sort of surprised me."

"Indeed," Artur said dryly. "I, also, was surprised to see your mouth on one of my subjects."

"I'm not one of your subjects. I mean it, Artur, cut that shit out right now. I was born in Quincy, for God's sake. I have American citizenship, okay?"

"Dual citizenship, it looks to me," Thomas said, ogling her tail.

"You are *not* helping."

"You may not put your mouth on her without my—ow."

"I'm trying not to stare but you guys keep giving me new things to look at. That punch, for example. Didn't it hurt like hell?"

"It did," Artur said, gingerly pressing the flesh below his eye.

"We have enough shit to worry about without this weird possessive streak of yours. If I want all twelve Boston Celtics to put their mouths on me, that's my business and not yours."

"Yeah," Thomas added.

"And *you*."

He leaned away from the tank. "If my theories on

differences in strength evolution between bipeds and mermaids are true, I really don't want you to slug me."

"You're not helping, either. Both of you, quit with the groping and the kissing." She had never, in her life, had to say such a thing. And she never, in her life, could have imagined the circumstances in which she was saying it.

"Then there is little for me to do," Artur teased.

"No, there's a lot. Artur noticed your little toxin problem," she said to Thomas. "I thought you guys could work together."

"Ummmm," Thomas said, eyeing Artur. "That's pretty interesting. I s'pose you guys would notice that stuff way before we did. What, you live around here?"

"No, I live on the other side of the planet. Some of our folk were in the area and reported what they sensed. When word reached my father, the High King, he set me this task."

"So the royal palace or coral reef or whatever is in the Black Sea?"

"Yes."

"I wonder why word took so long to—"

"There are only a million of us on the planet."

"Oh. Ah. Hmm. And with the planet being mostly water—"

"Exactly."

Exactly indeed. It explained why Fred had never bumped into another of her kind, though at one point she'd swum along the entire eastern sea shore. Telepathy, she supposed, could only reach so far.

"Then how—"

"You know, I just did this with Jonas not half an hour ago," Fred broke in. "You two run along and get acquainted."

They both frowned at her. "What are you talking about?"

"The question of my lodging has not yet been settled."

"Yeah, but now you have someone new to settle it with."

They frowned at each other, then turned their sour expressions back on her. She elaborated. "Uh . . . you guys team up, like Nick Nolte and Eddie Murphy. Or Owen Wilson and everybody. Solve the case. And

I'll—" *Get back to my life,* was her thought. Her nice, boring, controlled, uncomplicated life.

Why didn't it feel as appealing as it had this morning?

"But you have to help us," Thomas said at the exact same moment Artur commanded, "It ill becomes you to set aside your duty."

"Aw, no . . . not both of you at once . . ."

Thus followed a lecture, from both of them at once, about the sanctity of the seas and her duty as a scientist as well as a mermaid and how three heads were better than two and how her duty was to her prince and her career, yak-yak, until finally she was almost shouting, "All right, all *right*, I'll help, just cut it out!"

Thomas sat back and smiled. "Alrighty then."

Artur was also smiling, which wiped Thomas's smile away. "Yes, well said."

"So it's settled."

"Indeed; and well said."

Fred briefly toyed with the idea of leaping into the harbor, striking out for the horizon, and never looking back, not once.

Seventeen

"So here it is," Thomas announced, zipping his key card through the slot and throwing open the door to the Presidential Suite. "It's not home, but it's much. I stole that," he added cheerfully, "from Olivia Goldsmith, God rest her lipo'd soul."

Fred, raised by far-from-poor parents, and Artur, son of royalty, were both impressed, and said so.

Thomas shrugged. "Well, like I said my first day . . . You remember," he said to Fred. "I write romance novels."

"Of course I remember. It was—" She looked at her watch. "The day before yesterday."

"Right. Has it really only been two days?"

"Tell me about it," she muttered.

"Well, when I'm running around doing this stuff, I try to pay for my own lodging. It's not much to me, but sometimes it helps them. You know how the water programs . . ."

Fred nodded. At Artur's puzzled look, she elaborated. "A lot of the programs for water fellows got their government funding slashed. Or don't have much to begin with. Not just the water fellow programs, either. Just about every aquarium in the country depends on private contributions."

Artur's mouth thinned. "I was not aware, but I am not surprised." In unison, they said, "Bipeds."

"Now cut that out," Thomas said, tossing his key card on the eight-foot-long mahogany dining room table. "We're not all like that. I'm the one who came out here to try to fix the toxin problem, remember?"

"Congratulations," Artur said silkily, wandering around the suite. "One out of a thousand bipeds maintains awareness that the planet is not yours to ruin."

Fred snorted and Thomas said, "Now you're just being mean. Uh, the other bedroom is back there, on your left. There's another bathroom back there, too." As Artur disappeared from sight, Thomas beckoned.

Curious, Fred walked over to him. He put his warm hands on her shoulders, leaned down and whispered, "There's plenty of room for you, too."

She grabbed his hands, ignored his yelp of pain, and wrenched them off of her body. "Tempting, but no."

"Ow ow *ow*. I meant the couches are all fold outs."

"Oh, that's even more tempting. Sleeping on a bar while you two save the world, refreshed from sleeping on queen mattresses."

"King. And hey, I didn't want to team up with Aquaman," he growled. "That was your idea." Then he added hastily, "Not that I mind. I've got about a thousand questions for him. Think he'd let me run an MRI on him?"

"I doubt it. But go ahead and ask." Out of sorts,

and not really sure if she should stay or leave (and even more out of sorts that she was wondering . . . usually if she had to leave, she left, and didn't waste a second wondering about it, either), Fred wandered around the suite.

Gold brocade couches, ankle-deep carpet, dark wood everywhere, three phones that she could see, a bar, a plasma screen, four tables and a fireplace . . . and that was just the sitting room! She could just imagine the master bedroom.

"Little Rika," Artur called. "Come!"

Thomas sniggered. "You know, I just have to wait him out a day or two and—"

"And what?"

"Never mind."

With a warning glare over her shoulder, Fred stomped into the back. *The only reason I'm going is to show the other one that—what? I better think about this for a minute . . .*

"Do not call me like a dog," she began, pushing open the bathroom door. "And . . ." She fell silent. Artur, spectacularly nude (maybe there was something to her mom's "nudity is natural and beautiful" mantra), was standing, hands on his hips, in front of a double-head shower in a bathroom that looked slightly more complicated than the cockpit of Air Force One.

She prayed he knew how the toilet worked.

"I see the problem. Okay, you just turn this one here, and turn this one here . . ." She leaned in, felt his arms slip around her waist, sighed, adjusted the water level, grabbed the shower head, and squirted it at *his* head.

"Aaggghhkk! Very well, Little Rika, I will desist." He groped blindly and she handed him a towel. While he blotted, he added, "For now."

"Right. Well, you're all set up for a while. In fact, it was awfully nice of Thomas to let you stay in his suite—"

"I am aware of my responsibility to my host," he sulked. "I cannot help it if I preferred a different host."

"Great. Work on helping it. I'm going."

"Going?" Artur looked (and sounded) alarmed. "But there is sufficient room for you to stay."

"Yeah, finding a place to sleep isn't the problem."

"Then what is?"

She gave him a look.

He smiled. "Ah. That."

"Yeah. That. And so I bid you fond farewell, sweet prince."

"The words seem correct," he said suspiciously, "but the tone—"

"Can't put one over on you, handsome."

She turned and walked out, ignoring his hollered, "So you do find me pleasing to the eye?"

Meanwhile, Thomas had emptied his pockets. She suppressed a smile; he carried around more junk than a little kid. Cell phone, spare change (from several countries), money clip, string *(string?)*, earring (?), broken pencil, and T-pass. The debris was scattered all along a table she suspected was brought over on the *Niña*. He was jabbing at his cell phone but looked up when she walked in.

"Taking off?"

"Yes."

"Already?"

"Finally."

"I'll walk you to the door."

"The door's six feet away. I can find it."

"Now, what kind of a host would I be?" He hurried to her side. "Uh-oh."

"Name of all the gods, now what?"

"Check it out." He held something yellow over her head. "Mistletoe!" he said brightly, leaning in for a kiss. He caught her on the bottom of her chin, since she was looking up.

"That," she informed him, "is a leaf from a maple tree."

"It is?" the scientist asked. He yelped and leapt out of the way as she jerked the door open. "Aw, don't leave already. It's early. Hey, Artur! She's jamming!"

"I am aware," the prince's voice drifted out.

"See you tomorrow," Fred said and thought, to her credit, that she deserved full points for saying it without groaning.

Eighteen

🦄

Jonas got to the NEA just in time to hear Artur's roar.

"I detest this puttering about! I insist on action at once!"

Whoa. Jonas practically scampered over to the jellies exhibit, where Fred had promised the three of them would be when the NEA opened the next morning. He waved his pass at the elderly woman staffing the cash register and ran past the penguins, his nostrils flaring at the fish-poop smell he knew he wouldn't even notice five minutes from now.

Before he could triangulate their position from Artur's scream, he was waylaid by a little blonde cutie waving a schedule of events at him.

"Hi! Welcome to the NEA! Would you like a schedule for the seal shows?"

He slowed down for a look. What the hell; she *was* awfully pretty. A little shrill, and disturbingly bouncy, but mighty pleasant to look at.

"I've been here lots of times," he told her, noting the I Heart Dolphins pin over her left breast. Ah-ha! The annoying new intern Fred had bitched about. "I've pretty much got all the schedules memorized."

"It doesn't hurt to keep a reminder," she giggled, waving the paper at him.

"You must be one of the new interns."

"You bet! My name's Madison. Say, if you're so familiar with the place, maybe you could give me a tour." She giggled again, hiding her mouth with perfectly manicured fingers.

"Nice offer, but I'm supposed to meet a friend."

"Oh." She pouted. She was a good pouter, and he suspected she knew it. "Maybe next time."

"Yeah, maybe. Nice to meet you, Madison." He wondered how much time would pass before Fred strangled the poor girl, and gave her about seventy-two hours.

Hurrying away from the delectable intern, Jonas saw Fred, Artur and Thomas, and approached the group from behind. They were in a tight little huddle, Fred's hair shining like blue cotton candy under the ultraviolet lights, Artur and some other guy sort of blocking her—kind of protectively?

Jonas skidded to a halt and took another look. Hard to miss Artur with the height and the shoulders and the hair looking like it was on fire, especially now, with all the yelling. And hard to miss Fred, trying (unsuccessfully) to shush him, bony arms like windshield wipers as she held up her hands in a soothing, un-Fredlike way.

But the third guy filled up space just the same way those two did; almost as tall as Artur, almost as broad, dark instead of fiery but more intense, waving his arms around and trying to be heard over Artur's roars.

The new water fellow! So Fred had hooked them up, as she had planned. But was still stuck with them, which he knew was decidedly not in the plan.

Jonas stifled the urge to cackle. *Oh boy, oh boy! I didn't miss anything!* He raced up to the group, nearly trampling a busload of Girl Scouts.

"Hey," he panted. "What'd I miss?"

The small circle froze in midargument and turned to him.

"Well, the Prince of the Black Sea isn't a big believer in the scientific method," Fred began, blowing a lock of hair out of her eyes with an irritated puff. "Wanting instead to just jump in the harbor and start kicking ass. Because it's just that easy, don't you know."

"That is not what I—"

"And Thomas, here, thinks we need to do a tad bit more research first before we get an injunction, and when Artur found out an injunction was essentially a strongly worded piece of paper—"

He waved the rest of her explanation away. "Never mind. I get the gist." He stuck out a hand and the water fellow, looking bemused, shook it. "Hi. Jonas Carrey. Fred's best friend. Her oldest, best, dearest friend. The one from whom," he added, testing New Guy, "she has no secrets."

"I know they're Seafolk, if that's what you're getting at."

"Oh, good. Everyone's on the same page."

"I don't think everyone is," Fred grumbled. She was looking rumpled and out of sorts in a "Nantucket" T-shirt, cutoffs (the legs of which did not match in length, he noticed with an internal groan), and sandals. He shuddered at the state of her sandals, but as usual, Fred made it work. Or, rather, nobody looked at her clothes when they looked at her.

Certainly *these* two gents didn't give a crumbly crap that Fred was disheveled and hadn't had a pedicure since the first *Pirates of the Caribbean* hit DVD. In fact, they were looking at her the way Jonas looked at a plate of freshly steamed *edamame* sprinkled with sea salt.

He tried to intervene. "C'mon, Artur, you gotta give it more than half a day. The whole reason Dr. Pearson—"

"Thomas."

"—Tom—"

"Thomas."

"God, you've been around Fred a day and look what's happened to you! Okay, okay. Artur, the whole reason Thomas is on the team is so he can do all the grunt paperwork."

"Hey, thanks. You really know how to make a guy feel welcome. Why are *you* on the team?"

"Because we'd have to kill him to get him off," Fred muttered. She looked awful, even for Fred; now that he was closer he noticed the enomous dark circles, almost like bruises, under her eyes. He had a pretty good idea what had kept her up all night. "Don't knock it, Thomas. He can go out for sandwiches and stuff. He knows every waitress between here and Comm. Ave."

"That's true," he said modestly, inwardly bristling at being reduced to Sandwich Boy.

"This endless rambling grates on me unendurably."

"I gathered from the whining."

"Royal sons do not whine."

Thomas and Fred snorted in unison.

"Look, Artur, just give us another couple of days. We—" Fred looked around, motioned Jonas closer, and they all bent together in some sort of geeky, multispecies football huddle. "Thomas already has a bunch of the info compiled. We need to pinpoint the source; we can't just wade into the harbor and start kicking random ass."

"That's true," Jonas said. "Random ass is never a good thing. Though there was this girl from Revere once, who—"

"Then what am I to do in the meantime?" Artur had looked momentarily startled when Jonas and Fred each slung an arm around his shoulders and urged him to bend forward, but now his frustration was evident—more than evident, in his odd football huddle position. Jonas felt a stab of sympathy for the guy, who was probably used to wrestling great white sharks in his spare time. And he probably didn't like anything that would give Thomas an edge—even if it helped his cause. "This frittering is—"

"Yeah, we got that," Fred interrupted. "Look, this is all quite weird already, thank you. Don't do anything to make it—"

"Dr. Bimm?"

Fred audibly groaned, and Jonas inwardly cheered. An exciting morning, made even better by the appearance of the yummilicious . . .

He turned. "Dr. Barb!"

Dr. Barb looked startled at the volume of his greeting, and Jonas cursed himself. "Uh, hello, Jonas. Dr. Bimm. Dr. Pearson. Ah—" She tipped her head *way* back to look at Artur. "Sir, I couldn't help but notice your voice is scaring the—"

"That's why we came over to talk to him," Fred said.

"What?" Thomas asked. Then, "Right! Dr. Bimm and I, having no lives, came to work bright and early on a Saturday, but on the way to the labs, via the jellyfish exhibit on the other end of the building, we saw this guy making a ruckus, and came over to see if he needed to be escorted out." Then, lower, "Wouldn't bother me at all to kick his ass again."

"Oh." Dr. Barb looked slightly bewildered at both the glib response and the idea of Fred a) noticing a tourist, b) caring about a ruckus and c) then deciding to tend to the problem. "Ah. Good work, Dr. Pearson and, uh, Dr. Bimm, but we have, uh, security for that sort of thing."

Fred made a noise that sounded an awful lot like "ha."

An awkward silence fell. Around them, visitors were chatting and the din was pretty good, but the five of them were just looking at each other without a word. Even the glowing jellyfish bobbed around silently. In one of the curious silences that sometimes falls over a large crowd, Madison could be clearly heard to say, "Yes, I'm doing my paper on the dolphins in Boston Harbor."

Freshly distracted, Fred practically spat. "Good God!"

"Dr. Bimm."

"There *are* no dolphins in Boston Harbor!"

Dr. Barb sighed. "Dr. Bimm."

"How did that half-wit get in to Northeastern? And why the hell are we stuck with her?"

"Dr. Bimm. Remember, the NEA is heavily dependent on charitable donations."

Dr. Barb was practically dancing from one small black flat–clad foot to the other; he imagined she'd rather go for a quick jog around the lobster tank.

Then: "Why *are* you here this morning? Neither of you is on the schedule."

"Uh," Fred began, then looked at Jonas. It must have been a long night for all three of them, because they all looked a little helpless. "We—"

Jonas coughed. "Hey, Dr. Barb, you had breakfast yet?"

"I—what?"

"The first meal of the day? Start you off right? Give you sprinting energy through the lunch hour? Eggs? Bacon? Pancakes with real Vermont maple syrup?" As if there were any acceptable substitute in New England.

"I had a cup of yogurt," she replied, blinking up at him with her exotic, almond-shaped eyes. Oooooh,

131

he was getting that trembly/firm feeling he got whenever he talked to Dr. Barb. And not just because he knew he could give her a kick-ass makeover. "Nonfat."

"You call that breakfast?" he cried.

"Well. Yes."

"Ham and eggs, that's breakfast. Grits and anything, that's breakfast," he added, taking her by the elbow and trying not to be obvious about dragging her away from the group. "Eating nonfat yogurt is punishment for jaywalking, right? Come on, I know a great place right across the street."

"Well," she began, and it must have sounded so good she said it again. "Well . . . I couldn't be gone for long."

"Aw, who are you kidding? You probably weren't on the schedule for this morning, either."

"Well . . . I'm the one who draws up the schedule . . ."

"So cross yourself off it long enough to have a bagel with yours truly." He noticed her toes were practically skimming the tile and eased up, but didn't let go of her arm.

"Well . . . as I said, I couldn't be gone very long . . ."

"Right, right, place'd probably implode if you left for more than ninety minutes. We'll have you back in eighty-nine." *After Fred and the guys get lost.* "But you can't expect to go charging all over the NEA on yogurt. I thought you were smarter than that, Dr. Barb."

"I had no idea you were so worried about my welfare. Thank you, Jonas."

Jonas felt a thrill inside. Was it possible that Fred—dour, sour Fred—was shooting him the most grateful, sweetest smile of her life? *And* he was about to take his longtime crush on their first date?

This is the greatest day of my life! he thought, exalted, as he steered Dr. Barb past the throngs of tourists and students. He saw Madison's stare turn into a glare, but managed to give her a cheery wave. *And it's not even ten fifteen in the morning!*

Nineteen

𝕊

Barb Robinson was having a puzzling morning.

First, her dry cleaner hadn't had her eight lab coats ready, so she was down to three, low starch. Having so few symbols of her authority available to her made Barb extremely nervous. How was she expected to keep order at the NEA when everyone else there was so much smarter, younger

(better-looking)

and better educated? Answer: a crisp, blinding

white lab coat with her name (Dr. Barbara Robinson, Ph.D.) in red script over the left breast. She could feel her authority shoring up whenever her coat settled over her shoulders, when she buttoned it all the way to the top. She kept her long hair in a braid so everyone could see her name. So the volunteers and fellows could easily spot her.

You could, Barb had thought more than once, talk people into almost anything if you were wearing one of the things. It reeked of authority. The lab coat whispered to their subconscious, *trust me, do your work as diligently as I do, tell me your troubles, promise to work late on Friday.*

It was less effective, she thought wryly, in an Au Bon Pain.

"You want to take that off?" Dr. Bimm's nice gay friend said to her. He'd insisted on paying, almost like it was a real date, and had bought her a bagel with lox and cream cheese, and two milks. ("Dairy is dandy," Barb's nutritionist mother had been fond of saying.) "So you don't spill on it?"

"Oh, no. I'm fine. Thank you for breakfast."

Jonas gave her an odd look. "No big, Dr. Barb. You looked a little hassled."

"Oh. Well, you know. Saturday morning at the aquarium. Always a bit of a madhouse."

"Yeah, but it doesn't all need to be on your shoulders. I mean, you've got ticket takers and volunteers and stuff to worry about all that, right?"

"Well, I—yes. But the NEA is my responsibility."

"Boy, you and Fred," he muttered, working on his second chocolate croissant.

"Dr. Bimm is very dedicated to her work," Barb said proudly, for she had handpicked Dr. Bimm from a pool of several dozen highly qualified candidates, and had been justified in her decision many times over.

Of course, the odd punk hair made some of the fellows nervous, and Dr. Bimm wasn't the cheeriest employee she'd ever had, but her work was top quality and her devotion to duty was unwavering. She could think of no greater compliment to bestow upon anyone. "She is a credit to the NEA."

"Yeah, and two guesses when she had her last date." Jonas colored and Barb watched, puzzled, then realized Dr. Bimm's last date—oh, no. It couldn't have been—

"Not . . . Phillip?"

"Phillip," Jonas confirmed with his mouth full, lightly spraying her with crumbs.

"That was most likely a mistake," she admitted, taking another bite of her bagel. "But she seemed so—and we parted amicably enough—at least I did."

"If you don't mind me asking, what happened? Who'd be crazy enough to drop-kick somebody like you out of their marriage?"

Barb smiled, feeling a warm glow of pleasure. It was nice that Dr. Bimm's best

(only)

friend was so nice. It was a pure crying shame he was off the heterosexual market, with that blond hair and the incredible body which, she happened to know, he honed weekly in the dojo.

She had seen Madison flirting with him and felt sorry for the girl; she probably should have taken her aside and warned her, but Jonas's orientation was nobody's business. Certainly Madison's flirting was nobody's business also.

She realized he was waiting for an answer.

"I dumped him, actually."

"Oh."

"It was my fault, really. I just couldn't overlook all the sleeping around."

"*Oh.*" Jonas grinned. "Don't stop now. Dish!"

She found herself telling him. How they'd met at a fund-raiser for the NEA. Both in their late thirties, both ready to settle, both wanting to get married.

But *getting* married wasn't the same as *staying* married. Phillip had really wanted someone to go to events with, someone to be on his arm. A name on a mortgage application. The ability to check the "married" box on any form. Not a living, breathing, loving wife who expected him to stay out of other beds.

"The nerve!" Jonas mock-gasped. "You and your incredibly unrealistic expectations."

"Right," she said dryly, sipping her milk.

"What a dumbass! Man, if I'd known *that*, I never would have let Fred go out with him. No offense."

"None taken. But could you have prevented Dr. Bimm?"

"Well . . . she only went because—I mean, she didn't want you to—I dunno. It was, what? Six years ago?"

"About that, yes. Who is Dr. Bimm's new friend? The large man with the red hair?"

"Oh." Jonas's blue-eyed gaze went vague, and he waved off something invisible. "Just some guy from out of town. Let's get back to the dumbass you married. I mean, he's got you and he's out cheating?"

"Uh, yes. But I—" She looked down at her lap. She'd never see forty again, she didn't get much exercise, she was devoted to her work, and she had worn her hair the same way since ninth grade. Why *wouldn't* Phillip look for something a little

(younger)

fresher? Somebody like

(Madison)

a college student?

"I guess the thought of a long-term marriage just made him feel blue," she said, her smile fading. Blue made her think of Dr. Bimm's hair, and Dr. Bimm made her think of . . . "This man, he's from out of town, you say? How does he know Dr. Pearson? And why were they all—"

"Shit!" Jonas leapt out of his chair, and she saw the dark stain spreading across his shirt.

She jumped, too, grabbed her napkins and dabbed at him frantically. "Are you all right? Are you burned? Get that shirt off," she ordered. Coffee burns could be nasty, even after all the silliness with the suit against McDonald's. If she could get the hot cloth away from his skin in time, he might not be—

In response to her command, Jonas instantly stripped off his polo shirt, revealing a lightly furred chest, gorgeous pecs, nicely defined shoulders, and a by God six-pack set of abs.

She stared.

"I don't think I'm burned."

She stared.

"Dr. Barb? Am I burned?"

She stared some more.

He clicked his fingers in her face. "Dr. Barb? Come back now."

"My God," she said at last, almost shaking herself like a dog out of a pond. "I could grate cheese on your stomach."

"Uh—maybe later."

She inspected his skin closely and after a minute actually remembered why she was staring at his taut, muscular flesh.

"You're not burned," she assured him. *She* was feeling rather warm, but that was just too bad. Jonas was always nice, always seemed pleased to see her, was always hanging around Fred, was always lugging around Aveda bags and—

"Look, let's go up the street and hit Filene's. I need a new shirt, and you've got to let me do something about those lab coats."

—loved to shop.

It just wasn't fair.

Twenty

🦑

"Ah, Little Rika. At last I have you alone."

"Sshhhh!"

Fred had Artur by the hand and was leading him to the waterline. That was tricky at the NEA on Saturday mornings, as the place was jammed. She and Artur couldn't just strip in public and leap in.

"I do not understand why we do not merely leap in."

She rolled her eyes and they crept closer. They were beneath one of the observation decks, a glorified cement dock that, luckily, led straight to the water. With luck, they'd be twenty feet in and way deep and no one would see them.

"Look, Artur, you might not care if the entire world knows what you are, but I do. I managed to keep my secret from everybody until you got to town. I don't want anybody else finding out."

"You should not feel shame for—"

She swung around and let him feel the full force of her glare. "It's not about being ashamed!"

"It is."

"Like hell! It's about not wanting to spend the rest of my life as a zoo exhibit! Do you know what the bipeds would do to me?"

"No."

"You didn't see *Splash*, did you?" Of course he hadn't. Dumb question. Next! "You've seen what they do to the planet. You've seen the NEA. It's a nice cage for the fish, but it's still a cage. I like my freedom."

"If you were to come to my home, you would know nothing but freedom."

Now, why was that idea as exciting as it was terrifying? Just being able to swim around and do whatever, with her own personal tour guide none other than the High Prince.

"I like it here," she said shortly. Which was the truth. Right?

"You like hiding? You like being a commoner?"

"I come from a long line of commoners. Strip."

"Ah, you see, Little Rika? I am yours to command."

She smiled at him (she couldn't help it; he *was* kind of funny sometimes), kicked off her shoes, and started to take off her clothes. Above her, out of sight, she could hear the excited murmuring of NEA visitors looking at the outdoor exhibits.

Artur had been about to spontaneously combust, so she figured he was due for a break. And Thomas wanted more time to number crunch. She could have stayed to help Thomas, in fact had been sorely tempted, but in the end she decided to try the harbor herself. (Not to mention, there was no telling what mischief Artur might make if left alone.) Maybe she could smell or taste something in the water that would help. Artur's senses were no doubt much better instruments than hers, but she had the scientific background he lacked.

In fact, what was his background? Did they have colleges under water?

"What are you grinning about?"

"I cannot help feeling joy that you have chosen my company over his."

"Uh, it's not about that, Artur. It's just that the last time I was in the harbor I didn't notice anything was wrong, so this time—"

"Yes, yes." He waved her perfectly logical explanation away. "Whatever your rationale, you will be with me for the rest of the morning, while the biped pushes his papers around and makes numbers."

"Careful, pal. I was almost pushing papers and making numbers with him."

His smile widened. "My point. You are not."

"This isn't a contest, you know."

His smile slipped away and all at once he looked like the predator he was. "Everything is a contest."

"Hmmph. I am going to swim now. Try to resist the urge to take a chomp out of my butt."

"I shall try, but I make no promises."

She grinned; she couldn't help it. "Okay, that came out wrong." She dipped a toe into the water, then walked in a couple of feet, enjoying the breeze. She knew she felt chilly to other people, but one of the nice things about being a hybrid was that she didn't feel much cold. Which made sense, because there were plenty of places in the ocean that were *quite* cold. It was also the reason Jonas constantly gave her shit when she wore tank tops in November.

"Wasn't it great of Jonas to get my boss out of our way?" she said suddenly. "He really helped us out there."

"You choose your allies well."

"He's not an ally, he's my . . . you know. Jonas."

"As I said."

"He really took one for the team, taking Dr. Barb out for breakfast. I've worked for the woman for six years, and I've never seen her eat. It must be like taking your speech teacher out for drinks. Weird."

"That is for Jonas to fret about," Artur pointed out, slipping into the water beside her and easing out of sight. In her mind, he finished the thought: *Not you or I.*

"That's the team spirit," she muttered, and ducked under the water. It took a few seconds for her eyes to adjust—Boston Harbor wasn't exactly the clear azure of Cabo San Lucas. She kept a wary eye out for large clumps of seaweed—just the feel of the stuff on her skin made her . . . well, it made her skin crawl! And when it got in her *hair* . . . nightmare.

Maybe that's why she considered the sea a living thing, an entity all on its own. Because so much of it was so alive. Just swimming through it, she could feel how alive it was. It wasn't just the smell or the taste or the texture . . . or, rather, it was, but it was all of that and more.

She understood intellectually how the bipeds could use the ocean as a garbage dump, but could never get it emotionally. But then, they used the atmosphere as a garbage dump, too. You just couldn't count on any of them to—

She felt something clammy on her tail and shrieked. Uh, mentally. Artur let go of her and swam up beside her.

What ails you, Little Rika?

How did you get behind me? Oh, forget it. This. THIS ails me. She clawed at her hair. *Yeeesh!*

Our mother, our home? How can you be more comfortable in a sterile inland pool?

Two words: no seaweed.

Little Rika, you never cease to amaze. Or amuse. Ah! Nice to have room to breathe again.

Yeah, it's swell.

They swam together close to the bottom, avoiding the thousands of boats and ships that had turned the harbor into a saltwater highway.

I do not deny I have often wondered what it would be like to dance in the waves with you.

Was that—? It was! She snatched the clot of seaweed out of her way and threw it as hard as she could, which, fifteen feet under water, wasn't very.

Ick! Ick!

I admit, this is different from what I imagined.

Shut up. How could you "often wonder" anything? You haven't even been here three days yet.

My father knew his queen at once.

Bully for him. That doesn't have anything to do with me.

It could.

She chose to ignore that absurd statement and they swam in silence for a while. She swam ahead in a quick circle, then came back.

I don't smell anything so far. I mean, it's busy, you can tell it's the harbor and not the middle of the Caspian Sea; it's not exactly pure, but I'm not getting anything unusual.

The water here is not as fresh as I would like, but you are correct; neither is it poisoned. It may take us time to find the source. However will we pass the time?

Don't get any nutty ideas, Prince Grabby.

I cannot help it, Little Rika. Seeing you in your true element, your true form, with no interference from arrogant bipeds . . .

You've got nerve, calling anybody arrogant. She

stopped swimming and he nearly banged into her. They bobbed together for a moment and she told him, *When I have legs, that's my true form, too, Artur. Half 'n' half, except not as creamy. Er, that could have sounded sexier.*

He put his arms around her and kissed her gently, nothing at all like the bruising, possessive kiss from earlier. Perhaps because he didn't feel he had anything to prove in the water? Away from Thomas?

She let him. What the hell. She deserved a treat after the stressful week she'd had. And kissing Artur, no doubt about it, was a treat. She felt positively tiny in his arms, cradled, protected. She had the feeling that he could handle whatever problem came up: a great white, a sarcastic barracuda.

Ah, Rika, my Rika.

Shut up. More kissing.

He chuckled and obeyed, snuggling her into his embrace. At least he didn't point out that, this way at least, they could chat about current events the entire time they were making out and never miss a smooch.

She realized they were actually bobbing upside

down, but was too giddy from the kissing to care much. She felt the vibrations as one of the party yachts sped by above them, doubtless dragging more drunken tourists through the shit and—

No, she meant dragging them through the shitty harbor—shit! What was wrong with her?

Artur abruptly stopped kissing her. *Do you smell that?*

Smell it, of course I can smell it! She tried to spit. It didn't work. *I can taste it. Oh my God, I'm tasting shit!*

Artur grabbed her arm and flexed his tail, and they rocketed away from that particular spot. Despite his speed, despite his quick action, for a long, awful moment Fred was sure she was going to vomit. She struggled with the urge, thinking she must not, must not, must *not* barf in front of royalty. Not to mention, she hadn't barfed since the time she got drunk on Pepsi (a case) and vermouth (four bottles), and that had been over ten years ago. She had no plans to break her non-vomit streak.

And it was better now. She could still faintly smell

it, but suspected it was more imagination than fact. The way you could still smell dog shit once you've stepped in it, no matter how often you scrubbed your shoes.

Artur had gotten them away from the stream, or the bad spot, or whatever you wanted to call it, and he had done it with speedy efficiency . . . she wouldn't have been able to swim that fast with a speargun in her ear.

Thanks, Artur. That was pretty bad for a second.

I, too, had momentary discomfort.

Oh, thought Fred. Is that what they call it?

I can't ever come swimming here again . . . I'll always think I'm smelling shit even if I'm not. We gotta fix this.

Artur nodded. He didn't try to touch her, which she figured showed as well as anything how grossed out he was, too. *Thus my father's concern when he heard the news. I, too, feel the morning has been tainted.*

That was shit. I don't mean toxins. I don't mean poisons. She was swimming for the shore as quickly as she could, Artur keeping pace with no trouble. *I mean shit. Somebody's gonna pay. And I don't mean EPA fines, either. I mean pay through the NOSE.*

I quite agree, Little Rika . . . and it is a pleasant change to see your anger directed at a head other than my own.

It was shallow enough for her to stand, and she did, her legs as always forming without conscious thought. She shook her wet hair and managed to smile at him as he emerged beside her. "Some romantic swim, huh?"

He spat. "As I said. Not quite what I had envisioned."

Twenty-one

Thomas nearly jumped out of his skin when the door to his lab was thrown open and Fred, the mermaid of his dreams, snarled, "Some tin prick is throwing his shit into the harbor."

He turned away from the slides and microscope. Fred was splendidly drippy, her green hair plastered to her head, her T-shirt almost transparent in a couple of interesting places, her feet bare and pink and comely. She carried her shoes in one hand. The pretentious lug from the Black Sea, Artur, was looming behind her like a mugger, carrying his own shoes.

Where does he get clothing? Thomas wondered.

"Are you paying attention?" she demanded.

"Yeah, Fred, I know. It's why I'm here, remember?"

Fred stomped toward him. He wasn't sure whether to back up or try for a kiss. Since her hands were both in fists, he decided to compromise and stay where he was. He could hold his own in a fight, but he imagined Fred could rip him in half without much trouble.

And that redheaded bum, Artur, would be happy to help.

"You're not listening," she said, jabbing a bony finger at his chest. "Somebody is dumping his *shit* in the harbor. *Literal* shit."

"Oh, great," he groaned. "That's really nice. How lovely. Right into the harbor. Did you get a noseful?"

Her lips made an odd twisting motion, like she wanted to spit but was stopping herself. "I got a *mouthful*, feels like. It still feels like."

"All right. Well. I'm sorry to hear that, but it's actually helpful."

"How could you not know, with all your papers, what it was?" Artur demanded.

Thomas gave the lug a look. "It's a big ocean, Artur. And shit, for want of a better term, is all natural. It can be mixed up with a few things, I'm sorry to say." He took a breath and turned back to Fred. "Anyway, thanks for telling me this. I'm sorry you had to get a snootful, but at least it narrows down—"

"I figured. That's why we came to tell you."

"I was just over at City Hall and got copies of all building permits granted to anyone in a three-square-mile radius—" He gestured at the new pile of paper. "That, coupled with the fact that none of the Under-sea Folk noticed the, uh, shit until recently, and *you* didn't notice, and the fact that it's, you know, *shit*, makes me think it's a new building."

"Duh." Fred, his darling, looked annoyed she hadn't thought of it herself. "It's a hotel."

"Why do you think this?" the big red lug asked.

"New building by the harbor? That amount of

shit? It's a new hotel. They probably played fast and loose with the city council and now there's a pipe in the wrong place, dumping the crap of tourists into our harbor."

"A hotel like the building in which Thomas and I reside? A place strangers call home for a short period of time?"

"Yeah. And every room has a bathroom. And all that water—and what it takes away—has to go somewhere. It should go to a treatment plant first. Unless someone cut corners."

"Contrary to what they taught us in *Finding Nemo*, all pipes do not lead to the ocean. Unless you design them that way."

Artur looked revolted. "You bipeds never fail to astonish. Do you not realize—"

Thomas swallowed his annoyance, figuring that if the two of them had had to choke down shit earlier, he could hold his temper. "Stop lumping us into one category. I'd no sooner dump my own waste into a body of water than I'd run over a cat. *I'm* the one who showed up and told Fred the problem. *I'm* the one who's done all the research. *I'm* the one who spent the morning in City Hall. And *I'm* the one who's been at work while you two went off for a romantic swim."

"Poor you," Fred sneered. "I guarantee your morning wasn't as miserable as ours."

Artur looked wry. "I had thought it would be romantic, and it was. Until . . ."

Thomas almost smiled. He had not been happy, at all, when Fred had taken off with the big red lug, but at least the guy hadn't gotten very far during his alone time. Bad news: the guy was a prince. Good news: Fred didn't care. Bad news: the guy was huge and great looking and could show her a world the average person would never know. Good news: Fred didn't care.

Besides, Thomas figured, *I can show her a thing or two right here on dry land, I bet. And I won't give her crap for being half-and-half, like some of Artur's people would.*

Fred was picking through the plans piled on his desk, looking intrigued. Artur watched her, shifting his weight impatiently.

Ha! Got her. He knew the scientist in her couldn't stay away from the lab for long. Sure, Artur was a fellow Undersea Folk, but eight years of formal schooling left its mark, no matter if you grew a tail to swim or just put on swimming trunks from Target.

He watched her open up a plan and read it. Even from the back, she was breathtaking. Long, graceful limbs, and that hair . . . and that gorgeous, pretty tail. Green in some lights and blue in others, it was like a peacock tail, except a million times sexier.

He was aware that he had built Fred up in his mind because of what she was and not who she was. His mother had told him so many stories of mermaids that by the time he was ten, he was hopelessly besotted with the idea of jumping into the ocean and finding a friend who could follow his family all over the world.

Whereas his mother entertained him for hours with her wonderful stories (*The Little Mermaid*, *The Mermaid Wife*, *The Sea Morgan's Baby*), his father was simply not around much—he went where the navy sent him. And when you were the new kid and knew you'd be moving in another eight or ten or twelve months, there really wasn't much point in making friends.

So he read. And dreamed. And listened to stories. And *dreamed* . . .

Even before he knew Fred's secret, he was taken with her. She was the first woman scientist he'd ever met who wasn't, on a subconscious level at least, interested in male feedback. Or even aware the person she was interacting with *was* male. She was also the first woman—person—who wasn't paralyzed by conventional mores and standards of behavior. What she thought, she thought, and if people didn't like it, she didn't care. Or notice.

He blessed the impulse that had brought him back to work the night before, figuring he'd fight insomnia with toxin tables. And then he'd seen her, lazily swimming back and forth in Main One, her gorgeous blue-green tail shimmering, her long arms making graceful sweeping motions as she fed the fish, her green hair floating around her face in a gorgeous cloud that looked like liquid emeralds.

He had honestly thought, for a long moment, that his heart was going to stop. It just didn't seem possible. It was a hallucination brought on by fatigue and bad pizza. He had snapped under the pressure of not getting laid for seven months.

And then he'd stared some more. She didn't notice him right away, so he could look his fill. And he finally convinced himself: Fred, the cool, distant woman he'd met earlier, was a mermaid. An honest to God mermaid!

He couldn't help it: he'd raced to the top of the stairs and, once there, had to touch her. *Had* to. And once his hands were on her, his lips soon followed. Because here was the living embodiment of all his childhood fantasies, and he had no plans to let her go.

Ever.

And if a certain big red lug got in his way . . . well. He had a few ideas about how to stop a member of the Undersea Folk. And not just with aikido.

"Why don't you have a seat?" he said with forced

politeness to Artur. "It looks like Fred and I will be here for a while. You know, frittering with paperwork and other things you're bad at."

Artur gave him a black look, but said nothing.

"Careful," Fred warned. "That's your new roommate you're irritating. It'll make your nightcap together awkward."

He grimaced. He was already regretting the mad impulse that had prompted him to offer up his suite to Artur. Still, in his own way, he was fascinating, and Thomas had plenty of questions for the man.

Too bad they were rivals. He knew it. Artur knew it. Jonas even appeared to get it.

Everybody but the object of their adoration, who was even now bitching, "Thomas, is English your fourth language? I can barely read your writing."

"Shut up," he said warmly. "You've got bigger problems than my writing."

"Impossible," she said, looking alarmed.

"If it's a new hotel—let's see, who do we know who just popped up at the NEA whose parents are rich and own half the waterfont?"

Now she was looking positively revolted. "No."

"There is a suspect?" Artur asked.

"No," Fred snapped.

"I'm just saying," Thomas added.

"No."

"It wouldn't hurt to talk to her."

Fred grimaced. "Obviously you haven't talked to her."

"Oh, I have, honey, believe me. She threw a pass at me that nearly knocked me unconscious with its subtlety."

"How awful for you," Fred sneered.

He ignored the sarcasm. "That whole 'look at me, I'm a sub-human twit' thing could be a front."

"Olivier wasn't that good an actor."

"Have it your way. But you have to admit, it's an interesting coincidence. And talking to Madison Fehr can't be worse than sucking down shit." Her glare was so sizzling, he nearly flinched, and changed the subject. "I'm getting pretty hungry. Are you guys?"

Both Undersea Folk looked positively ill.

"Oh. Sorry. Yeah, that'd put me off my feed for a

while, too. But I can't help being hungry. It's lunchtime."

"Well, Jonas can run out and get you something . . ." Fred suddenly looked around, then looked at her watch. "Where the hell *is* Jonas? Not still with Dr. Barb, I hope. Poor guy."

Thomas thought of the way Jonas had run off with Dr. Barb, who was in awfully good shape and pretty young to be running the NEA, and didn't think the guy had it so bad at all.

"Hey, Artur. Maybe you could get me a sandwich." He couldn't resist.

He chuckled at the prince's expression, deciding it was worth Fred's sigh of exasperation. Yes, the day was definitely looking up.

Twenty-two

🦄

"Okay, come out."

"Jonas, I can't."

"Will you come out already? How can I tell you how it looks if you won't let me see?"

"I'll tell you how it looks. It looks silly."

"I'll be the judge of that, Dr. Lab Coat. Out."

Blushing to her eyebrows, Dr. Barb pushed open the dressing room door and stepped into the tiny hallway. She was wearing one of the four outfits Jonas had bullied her into trying on and, in his opinion, the most flattering.

It was a navy two-piece suit, the skirt falling softly just above the knee, the jacket double-breasted and held together in the middle by one big button. And it was a Givenchy. *On sale!*

Jonas stared at the button. "We have to pick out a bra in the same color as the jacket."

"No we do *not*. Jonas, I feel half naked in this thing! You can see my brassiere, for heaven's sake."

"News flash, Dr. Barb: people stopped saying brassiere forty years ago."

"I'm trying to be an authority figure not a—a Playmate of the Month."

"Barb, bras are trendy right now. Women are buying strappy tees and then buying bras so they can co-ordinate. And don't forget the whale-tail trend—you know, when you can see a woman's thong above the waistline of her jeans?"

"That," she said firmly, "was a trend for the young."

"Well, the young can't afford this suit. Showing an

inch of the front of your bra is hardly the same as forgetting to wear shorts and bending over a tractor to be Miss February."

Her face went, if possible, even redder, and without a word she turned around to duck back inside the changing room, but he caught her by the elbow and gently pulled her back. "Come on, let me get a good look," he coaxed. "I think it's fabulous. Let me tell you why."

He led her to the three mirrors at the end of the room. "See, the skirt is long enough so you don't look like an escapee from the *Ally McBeal* set, but short enough to show off your legs. You have really terrific legs. And the color is awesome. Brings out your eyes, puts some color in your cheeks, even brightens up your hair. Which we'll get to in a minute. Now, the jacket . . . wrist-length sleeves, but not too much padding in the shoulders, so you don't look like you've OD'd on *I Love the 80s*. The cut in the front really doesn't show much skin. See, you could wear this under an open—*open*—lab coat and look like a million bucks, and still be the boss, and show everybody how gorgeous you are at the same time."

She tried to pull away. "Oh, Jonas, you're sweet, but I'm not—"

"That is a gorgeous forty-year-old woman in there," he said, not letting go of her arm, and pointing to the mirror with his other hand. "Sexy and smart and The Boss. I mean, what could possibly be hotter than that?"

"Forty-five. As my ex never failed to remind me," she added, a little bitterly, "I'm never going to see thirty again."

"Fuck your ex. I think this is the one. We should get this one. And a matching bra."

Dr. Barb stared at herself for a long minute. "Well. The color *is* nice."

"The color is fucking phenomenal, I'm telling you, it brings out all your natural color, brightens up your—oh, right. Your hair."

She clutched her braid and tried to back away. "Never mind my hair."

"Come on, Dr. Barb. All I'm asking is that you cut two feet off of it."

"No!"

"But it would look *so* much better if it wasn't dragging your whole face down. I'm thinking layers around your face, and shoulder length. And," he added slyly, "everybody could still read your name on the coat."

"No, Jonas. No. Not the hair."

"Yes, the hair, listen, trust me. I'm an impartial observer. Besides, you think I do this for every woman?"

"Certainly you've never done it for Dr. Bimm," she said slyly, and he laughed. She looked at the mirror, and it was almost like his laughing reflection helped her make up her mind. "All right. I'll take it. But when the board fires me for dressing like a slut, I'm moving in with you."

"Done," he said fervently. "Okay, hurry up. We've got time to hit the lingerie counter and then it'll be lunchtime."

"*Lunch*time?" Dr. Barb practically shrieked, looking at her watch. "Oh, Lord! I should have been back—"

"Dr. Barb, what in the world is the use of being

The Boss if you can't fuck off for a Saturday? I mean, a *Saturday*. Come on."

"You are very bad for me, Jonas," she scolded, stepping into the dressing room and (rats!) closing the door. "You are a bad, bad boy."

He leaned against the wall so he wouldn't fall down. God, he loved the older teacher type thing she had going, but when she *scolded* him! He hoped to God she didn't notice the raging boner lurking in his boxers.

"I never even let Phillip pick out my clothes," she said from the other side of the door, and laughed. "I can't imagine what he'd think of this."

"He'd think 'when did I turn into the world's biggest dumb shit?' is what he'd think."

She laughed and he heard the sound of rustling clothing. He squashed the urge to mash his ear against the door and imagine what she was putting on. Or taking off. "Considering the fact that you never had the pleasure of meeting him, you certainly have strong opinions about him!"

"He's a dumbass. Anybody who'd let you go isn't worth a nanosecond of my time. Or yours."

"Oh, Jonas," she sighed. There was more of that tantalizing rustling. "You're so very good for my ego!"

Twenty-three

ॐ

"Dr. Bimm is lucky to have a friend like you." Dr. Barb was saying over arctic char half an hour later. They were at the Legal's right by the NEA, within sight of the building in her charge. As long as she was sitting where she could see tourists weren't stampeding out, or the building wasn't collapsing in flames, she was almost relaxed. "It was so sweet of you to take me shopping. Especially when you were the one who needed a new shirt."

Note to self: Fred owes me a new shirt. I ruined a

Ralph Lauren polo for that ungrateful harpy! "Yeah, well, I was free. And it was fun. I love to shop. And I got three new shirts out of it, too." Dr. Barb had insisted on paying for his clothes, even though he'd dumped his coffee on himself on purpose. And Fred *still* owed him a new shirt. He could have been scalded to death!

"I don't understand how it's possible for a man like you to have a free Saturday. Why haven't you ever settled down, Jonas? Too young?"

He laughed. "You're talking like you're ready for a nursing home. You've only got about fifteen years on me."

Dr. Barb looked away. "Ah—don't remind me. But let's get back to you. Why hasn't someone snapped you up?"

"Well. I've been—I mean, you know, I see people. I get out. A helluva lot more than you NEA geeks, that's for sure."

She raised an eyebrow at him. "I think you should set your goals a bit higher."

He laughed again. "Right, right." The waitress

brought him his appletini and a ginger ale for Dr. Barb. They clinked glasses. "To the new, sexy, awesomely gorgeous you, who really isn't new, but now other people will figure it out, too."

She blushed—God, he didn't know women still *did* that!—and they clinked glasses again. Then he resumed the chatter that either irritated Fred or bored the hell out of her, but which the luscious Dr. Barb appeared to find fascinating.

"Anyway, I see people and go out and there's always a party going on and stuff like that, but I just, you know, haven't found that special someone."

"That's amazing to me. You must have people lining up."

"Well . . . I don't know about that . . . but I've kind of got a crush on someone. So it makes it hard to want to get to know someone *else*, get it?"

Dr. Barb nodded. "Of course, I understand perfectly. What is that you're drinking? It's the color of lamb jelly."

"Appletini. Try."

She picked up his glass and took a sip, raised her

eyebrows, and took another one. "Oh. That's wonderful! I'll have one when I'm not working."

"You're *not* working today, Dr. Barb."

She giggled. *Giggled.* He thought it was adorable. He wanted her to do it again. *Maybe if I juggled?* "Oh yes I am. I'm going back after lunch."

"You can't. After lunch we're going to Sergei's."

"Who?"

"Only the hottest stylist in town right now, booked for months, but he owes me a favor—I introduced him to his husband—so he'll see you. And he'll give you a discount on the cut."

She shook her head and set his glass down. "No, Jonas. No haircut. No Sergei."

"But you're so close to goddess-hood!" he wailed.

"Goddess-hood? Oh, Jonas. We have to stop. You're going to give me a swelled head. Soon I'll forget I'm a middle-aged frump and then where would we be?"

He stared at her. "Frump? *Frump?*" he repeated, incredulous. Okay, maybe that last one was a little loud; the table in front of them turned to look.

"Dr. Barb, when we were in that department store with all the mirrors, did you bother to look in any of them? You're as far from a frump as—as—" He groped for a simile. Or was it a metaphor? "As Fred is from Miss Congeniality."

She reached across the table and took his hand. Took. His. *Hand!* "Jonas, you're so sweet. You've given my ego such a boost, I can't thank you enough. And I'm thrilled that you see me that way, really I am, even if I can't quite make that leap myself. Now, you've done so much for me, I'd like to do something for you. Tell me about this crush you have. Maybe we can get you hooked up, as the kids say."

Oh. Gulp. "Well . . . I've known this person for years but haven't really screwed up the courage to get to know them very well. I can hardly even be in the same room—you know how it is."

Dr. Barb nodded. "Now, Jonas, you listen to me."

"Sterner."

She looked puzzled, but raised and hardened her voice. "Now, Jonas, you listen to me." He got all tingly when she used her schoolteacher voice. "You are a wonderful guy: handsome, funny, smart, sweet. You're going to make some man very happy. The trick is finding Mr. Right, as they say."

"What?"

"You've got a lot to offer some lucky fellow, and I'm sure the gentleman you've got a crush on will see that if you can just get to know him a little better."

"But—" In his surprise, he blurted out the truth. "But *you're* the gentleman I've got a crush on!"

They stared at each other. Dr. Barb froze with her ginger ale halfway to her mouth. And Jonas cursed himself. This wasn't the first time a woman had assumed he was gay, but he never dreamed that Dr. Barb would think— Couldn't she tell he could hardly keep his hands— Couldn't she *tell*?

"But—you're gay. You're Dr. Bimm's gay best friend."

"I'm not gay."

"But you are."

"Dr. Barb," he snapped, "I think I would know, okay? Trust me, I'm not even bi. I'm just very very very secure in my masculinity, okay?"

Color began to climb in her face. "But—you like to—"

"Metrosexual."

"But you also like—"

"Secure in my masculinity."

Now she was red faced and stammering. "But I—I never s-see you w-with any girls—women, I mean—"

"You've never seen me with anybody."

She closed her mouth so quickly, he heard the click of her teeth coming together. When she spoke, her voice was very small and she sort of breathed the whole thing out, really fast.

"YoumeanI'mtheoneyou'vehadacrushonallthis-time?"

"Sure. I liked you the first time I saw you, even though you were wearing that awful green pantsuit under your lab coat."

"But Jonas—I'm so much older than—"

He snorted. "Fifteen years—"

"Sixteen, I believe."

"Big deal, that hardly makes you Methuselah. And I *love* older women. Love. Them. Especially really smart ones. Especially authority figures. Especially—never mind, I think you've had enough shocks for one day."

"It's just that I never—I mean, Fred never—and I never had—I mean you never said—I mean—" She was looking around wildly, possibly for the fire exit.

"Believe it or not, I know what you're thinking. You thought you were having a totally platonic sexual tension free morning with a gay guy who would never ever have sex with you, and now that you're replaying the morning, you've realized we were actually on a date and I saw your bra in the dressing room."

She was spry, that Dr. Barb. She was on her feet and he hadn't seen her move. "No, I'm—it's impossible. It's just not possible." She threw her napkin down on the table.

"Which part? The part where I've been crushing on you for six years, or the fact that you've been the object of my fantasies? Or the part where I think you're hot and gorgeous? Or the part where I'm not crushing on Colin Farrell instead of you?"

But he was talking to nobody. She had turned and run out of the restaurant.

"Waitress! Three more, please."

He laid his head on the table, pulled out his cell and stabbed Fred's number.

"What?"

"Dr. Barb's on her way back."

"Okay. We've done about all we can here, anyway. Everybody wants to break for something to eat. Wanna come?"

"Frankly, no."

"Oh. Are you all right? You sound kind of . . . hollow."

"My heart has been stomped on."

"So no lunch then?"

"No."

"Okay, well, bye."

Fred hung up. He didn't hold it against her. It just wasn't in her nature, when she was working on a thorny problem, to notice anything else. Or anyone else.

Besides, for once in his life, he had no urge to tell Fred anything. At all.

Twenty-four

Fred hung up. "He sounded weird."

"I've just met him, but are you surprised?"

"No, really, even for Jonas." She shrugged. She had enough problems right now. "I'll talk to him later. He'll magically show up and find me, probably when I least expect it. That's his superpower."

"Ah. I wondered if bipeds had any abilities beyond destruction."

"Well," Thomas said cheerfully, opening the door

for Fred, "some of us can toss princes ass over teaket-
tle into fish tanks."

Fred snickered; she couldn't help it—it *had* been
funny. Thomas stepped in behind her, neatly cutting
Artur off so that he nearly walked into the door frame.
Artur in turn gave Thomas a "friendly" shove—and he
nearly went sprawling into the wall.

She turned and frowned. "Play nice, you two."

"What?" Thomas said innocently.

"Little Rika, you have a suspicious mind."

"I have a headache from the trouble you two are
causing, not to mention all the shit that's probably
still in my lungs." That was a small lie; she didn't
have a headache. She never got sick. But still. They
were driving her to one, and that was bad enough.

"Legal's okay?" Thomas was asking, shouldering
into a leather jacket. "Or do you want to go back to
that sushi place? Art? You need raw fish?"

"No. I can eat many of your foods."

"Uh, you guys—aren't you going to be cold? I
mean, it's probably only sixty degrees outside today."
He gestured to their T-shirts and shorts.

Fred and Artur looked at each other, then at Thomas. "No."

"Oh. Right. Well then. Fancy? Or fast? Raw or cooked? Or Souper Salad? Subway? Clam Shack?"

"Let's go to Faneuil Hall," Fred suggested. "Artur can get a look at all kinds of stuff. And there's bound to be something there for all three of us." Also: she loved Faneuil Hall. Well. The food. Not the crowds.

It was only a few blocks from the NEA, and they were there after five minutes of brisk walking. Brisk walking in silence, Fred was relieved to see. She felt exhausted: not just physically—in fact, not physically at all—her brain was tired. Being around Artur and Thomas was like walking a tightrope. Made of glass. In bare feet.

And their little shit problem—when she got hold of the nasty fuck who was dumping his crap into the ocean, they were going to have a long talk. Possibly in the ICU.

The sights and smells of Faneuil Hall lifted her spirits, and she quickened her step so that she was almost running to the food stalls. Even better, at this time of day, it was hardly even that crowded.

"Is this a gathering place for your people?"

"Only the hungry ones."

Artur sniffed appreciatively. "I smell . . ."

"Everything."

"Everything?"

"Pretzels, steamed clams, clam chowder, hamburgers, turkey legs, ice cream, sushi, gelato, bagels, doughnuts, pizza, chocolate chip cookies, milk." Fred took a breath. "Smoothies, rice, curry, noodles, frozen yogurt, lemonade, enchiladas, milkshakes."

The marketplace was brilliantly lit, and they went into the main building, which, from one end to the other, was stall after stall of food.

"Great oceans," Artur gasped. "I have never seen so much food in one place!"

"Do you guys even cook your food?" Thomas asked. He tried to sound idly curious, but Fred wasn't fooled; there was barely contained eagerness there for anyone who cared to see it.

"At times we collect on land and have feasts, yes.

The ones who can build and control fire are revered in our culture."

"I'll bet."

"But never in all my years—"

"How old are you, anyway?"

"I have forty-nine years," Artur answered absently, his gaze shifting from Steve's Greek Cuisine to La Pastaria.

"For . . . forty-*nine*? As in, almost fifty?" Fred was shocked. If asked, she would have put Artur at early thirties. "Wow! You're way older than I am."

"That makes sense, though." Thomas put his big warm hand on her face. "Cool to the touch. I bet your BP's in the basement, too. Sluggish heartbeat. And all that time in the water, of course. Keeps you looking young. Because you don't look twenty-nine, gorgeous. Not even close."

"How'd you know how old I was?"

"Took the time to find out," he said carelessly, like it was no big deal. Like it wasn't borderline stalking.

She took his hand away and gave him a look. "Well. It's true, I get carded everywhere I go. But—"

"You know, Fred, I think it's great that you don't look your age. I mean, I don't care how old you are. I wouldn't care if you were an ancient, drooling, doddering old man like Artur is."

She grinned. "Watch it, pal. You may have flipped him once; but I get the idea you might have gotten lucky that first time."

"Not lucky enough. You were naked, as I recall."

"Thomas. I didn't have legs. And, by necessity, the place between them."

"A guy can dream, can't he?"

She laughed. "I can't tell if you're open-minded or just a pervert."

He edged closer. "Find out," he said, his breath warm on her lips. She couldn't help it; she closed her eyes and moved closer to his warmth, and—

"You two! Come at once! I require a King Corn Dog!"

Thomas groaned and backed off. "Honey, I thought we were going to get a sitter for the baby."

She snorted and trotted after Artur. He was standing in the middle of the walkway (bad Faneuil etiquette, but she'd tell him later) staring wildly all around. It almost looked like he wanted to try everything at—

"I also require a bread bowl of clam chowder and a fruit cup and a Frappuccino and an éclair."

"Jeez, Artur, I didn't win the lottery on the way over here. Hey, rich romance novelist! Get over here!"

"Oh, bad enough he's living with me? I have to pay to feed him, too?"

"Produce the money items from your clothing," Artur commanded. "I shall start with the éclair."

It was great fun watching Artur sample everything from coffee-flavored gelato to a chicken sandwich. He had a stomach of iron and was inexhaustible. He even wore Thomas out; the guy finally just handed Artur a bunch of twenties and sat back to watch.

"You don't have any allergies that I as your roommate should know about, do you?" Thomas asked, nervously watching Artur slurp down another Frappuccino.

"By my father's name, this food is fit for a king! I ought to know. What is this?"

"Lo mein."

"And this?"

"A sugar cookie."

"And this?"

"A lobster roll."

"And this?"

"A slice of pepperoni pizza."

"Mmmph," Artur said. He had pretty good table manners for a man mastering eight cuisines at once.

"I have to admit," Thomas said, grinning, "this is a shitload more fun than I thought it was going to be. Wait 'til he discovers room service."

"Don't say 'shit,'" Fred groaned. She picked at her salad. "My appetite was almost coming back."

Artur shoved a lobster roll under her nose and she recoiled. "Artur, I'm allergic! I'll puke for half an hour if I eat that thing."

"Little Rika, you do not know what riches you deny yourself." A small bit of lobster roll hit Fred on the left cheek; she brushed it away. "I wish the High King were here. He loves a fine feast."

"Maybe you should go home," Thomas suggested

with all the subtlety of a sledgehammer. "I mean, to bring him back for a visit. Someday."

"Someday, perhaps." Artur was in too good a mood to be baited. "Again my thanks, good host."

Thomas waved it away. "Glad you're enjoying it. They open in the morning, in case you want to come back for breakfast."

"Ah. Breakfast!"

Fred smirked and forked a cherry tomato into her mouth.

Twenty-five

The next morning, Fred grimly followed the sound of the singing. It was (ugh!) "Part of Your World" from the Disney (ugh!) soundtrack. The voice was a perfectly on-key soprano, pleasant and carrying, and Fred followed it all the way up the stairs to the top level of Main One. It was after hours, and, thank heavens—no crowds. But it also meant that she had Madison (bleah) to herself.

At the top of the tank she found Madison, leaning over the edge and crooning to the fish.

"Stop that immediately," she ordered, resisting the urge to clock the woman on the side of the head with the bucket of fish.

Madison jumped. "Oh! Hi, Dr. Bimm! I didn't hear you come up. You're rilly rilly quiet."

"How could you hear anything over all that yowling? What are you doing?"

"Oh, it's one of my theories, like," the girl explained helpfully, dressed in a pink shell top and a miniskirt so brief it looked like linen panties. *Real* appropriate for the workplace. "I think the fish do better if they can hear pleasant things like music 'n' stuff."

Know any Pet Shop Boys? "Yeah, that's . . . yeah." She peered into Main One and dropped a smelt, which was quickly scooped up by a passing barracuda. Excellent. The strike, brief as it was, appeared to be over. She'd pop into her scuba suit after she finished interrogating the idiot and feed them properly.

The idiot was talking; better pay attention.

"You're the marine biologist, Dr. Bimm. What do you think?" She blinked her big blue eyes at Fred and twisted a blonde curl around one finger.

"About what?"

"About singing to the fish. Do you think it helps them?"

You don't want to know what I think. "So, your parents are rich, huh?" She cursed herself; Thomas would be better at this. And Jonas would be masterful at it. But the crumb had disappeared and Thomas was ass-deep in lab work. And Artur would probably scare the hell out of this twit. "Old Boston family and all that?"

"Umm-hmm."

"So what brings you here?"

Her big blue eyes got, if possible, bigger. "Oh, Dr. Bimm, I've just wanted to work with dolphins since I was just a kid."

"Since the Dark Ages, huh?" Fred watched the younger woman dabble her long pink fingers in the water. *Hope one of the turtles mistakes those for shrimp,* she thought viciously. "You're aware there are no dolphins at the NEA?"

"Huh?"

"There. Are. No. Dolphins. At the NEA." *You. Fucking. Idiot.*

Madison smirked. "Not yet."

"Oh." Fred thought that one over. "Your folks are buying you dolphins and plunking them into a new tank in the NEA?"

"After they fund the new habitat."

That made sense. It was stupid, but it made sense. "So that's why you're here?"

"Of course!"

"But what if it takes longer than the length of your internship?"

"Oh, Dr. Barb said I could, like, volunteer here as a long as I wanted."

"Of course she did. Your folks haven't, uh, built a new hotel and designed the bathroom pipelines to empty into the bay, have they?"

"Ewwwwwwwwwwwww!"

"Interview over," Fred said, bored, and left. The strains of "Part of Your World" followed her all the way down the stairs, out the door and onto the cobblestones.

Twenty-six

🐚

She pounded on Jonas's door for the third time, pressed her ear to the wood, and—yep, she was positive. Someone was rustling around inside.

"Jonas, open the damned door! It's been three days! If I find you dead in there it's going to be a *huge* inconvenience for me!"

More sinister rustling.

"Jonas! You have until I count to one. Then I'm kicking your door in and you'll lose your security deposit. Ready? One—"

She raised a foot just as the door swung wide. Jonas stood there, wrapped in the goose down quilt from his bed. His blond hair stood up in clumps, not the carefully moussed waves he usually spent hours coaxing to life. His eyes were bloodshot. And for the first time in recorded history, he wasn't wearing Aramis cologne.

"My God. You look like the run half of a hit and run. Where the hell have you been?"

"Dying," he said hollowly.

"Well, it's going around because Dr. Barb's got it, too."

She'd been following him past piles of takeout boxes and nearly walked into him when he stopped short. "She has? I mean, she hasn't been coming to work?"

"Yeah. Which makes it easier to sneak the guys in, but it's seriously weird not having her there. Nobody can remember her ever being sick. I mean, it's gotta be a plague of some sort."

"Of some sort," he mumbled.

"God, it reeks in here. You've got some explaining

to do, chum. How could you disappear for three whole days like that? Artur and Thomas have been driving me up a goddamned tree."

"Leave me alone," he moaned, plopping facedown onto his couch. "Can't you see I'm dying?"

"You're not dying. You're sulking. What's wrong, did Sergei pack up his salon and leave town? Did Ralph Lauren stop making shirts?"

"Worse," he said hollowly.

Fred was stymied. Jonas didn't have problems. Ever. She was the one who was often plunged into despair.

She played the guilt card. "You haven't called, you haven't come around—I was half afraid you had left town without saying anything to me."

"Sorry."

Time for the sympathy card. "Uh—cheer up?"

"I appreciate the effort, Fred. Go away now."

She prowled around the living room, racking her brain. "Uh—want some breakfast?"

"No."

"Come on. Pull yourself together. Whatever it is, it's not any worse than my problems. It can't be."

He sighed and rolled over to face her. "Fred, just because they're not your problems doesn't mean they're not problems."

"Oh yeah? Try this on for size. If Thomas isn't trying to steal kisses, Artur is. And Artur is going to blow pretty soon; we've been spending a lot of time in the lab because I have zero interest in jumping into the shithole that is Boston Harbor."

"What?"

"See? If you'd been hanging around you'd know. The mysterious toxins? It's shit."

"You mean—literally?"

"Oh yeah. Gah, I can still smell it. So we've been going through permit paperwork and toxin reports and all that happy crappy—literal happy crappy, I guess—and we finally narrowed it down to a couple of suspects, one of which I was able to eliminate, but not until I'd heard way too much singing, and now, I'm sorry to say, we're taking the *Lollipop* out today."

He looked alarmed. "Fred, you can't get on a boat."

"I know."

"You're terrible on boats!"

"I tried to tell them. But the alternative is letting them go alone, and they'll probably beat each other to death."

"Your love life is twice as exciting as mine."

"This kind of excitement I can do without. And they're not in love with me. It's just an infatuation."

"Sure it is."

"Don't start that whole 'Fred dismisses love because she has a fear of abandonment' bull again."

"But you do. And you do." Jonas stared at the ceiling. "I'm in love. I finally told her."

"And?" Fred assumed it was going to be awkward.

"She ran out. *Ran.*"

"Oh, ouch. Who is this bim? Just point her out. See how well she can run when I break both her legs."

He sighed. "Tempting, for all sorts of reasons, but never mind."

"Well, forget the loser. Whoever she is, you can do better."

"She's not a loser," he snapped, showing signs of life. "Don't call her that again."

"Jonas, if she couldn't see how wonderful you are, she's a big fat stupid giant loser and I never plan to call her anything else."

"I've been in love with her for six years."

"Uh—time heals all wounds?"

"Nice try."

"Look, clean yourself up and come down to the NEA with me. It'll do you good to get out. And I could really use your help. You're so good at distracting the guys from hurting each other."

He sighed again. "I can't."

"How come?"

"I don't have any underwear."

"Since when," she demanded, "do you feel the need to wear underwear every day?"

He thought about that for a moment. Then: "Point." And went to take a shower.

Twenty-seven

The *Lollipop* was moored at the NEA dock beside the *Voyager III*, which tourists used for whale watches. Much smaller, the *Lollipop*—

"As in, 'the good ship'?" Jonas asked. "Get it? No? Never mind."

—was for the aquarium's scientific expeditions and research. As a water fellow, Thomas could sign it out and commandeer the crew whenever he wished; so could Fred.

With Dr. Barb's permission, of course. But she

wasn't around, so they dodged that bureaucratic bullet nicely.

"See?" she said, forcing cheer that sounded unnatural. "Isn't it nice to be out on this beautiful, um, autumn day?"

"It's raining." Jonas turned up his coat collar.

"Oh, a little water won't hurt you. Take it from me. At least you're getting some fresh air. Want to come on the boat?"

"With you?" He shuddered, the insensitive creep. "Absolutely not. No way. No. I'm only here because you bullied me out of my safe cocoon. Once I bid you toodle-loo, I'm sinking back into despair."

"I promise I'll sit in one spot and not move."

"Fred. No."

"Okay, okay. It's probably all for the best."

They heard clomping noises at the far end of the dock and turned to see Artur and Thomas heading toward them.

"Oh, like Undersea Folk never take a shit in the ocean!"

"Our shit, as you put it, breaks down when

exposed to seawater. Certainly we do not pump concentrated loads of it into our living room."

"I've had about enough of the smug routine, Artur. Show me the living breathing person who never screws up and I'll show you nobody alive on the planet."

"But surely you agree that your kind 'screws up' at a level unsurpassed by any other species. And many who 'screw up' aren't in fact making a mistake at all. They do it purposefully, and generally for the sake of conquest."

"Profit, really."

"Same thing."

"A million Undersea Folk running around the oceans eating all the raw fish they can get their hands on, and you guys aren't causing *any* damage?"

"You did not know of our existence until this week."

"Yeah, but every culture has mermaid legends. They sprang from somewhere, pal. People didn't just pull the stories out of their asses. And you guys probably control those krakens that yanked all those seventeeth-century European ships into the water, killing—"

"I tire of this topic."

"Tough nuts. We—"

"Ah, my boys," Fred said with mock fondness. "What would I do without them? They've quit with testing each other physically, so now it's debate, debate, debate. Kill me now."

"You don't get off that lucky," Jonas muttered.

Fred was about to retort when her cell rang. Irritably, she plucked it off her hip and flipped it open. "Yeah?"

"Dr. Bimm?" It was Dr. Barb. "I see by the sheet that you and Thomas are signing out the *Lollipop* today."

Oops. "Yeah."

"I think, in light of what happened last time, I feel strongly that—wait. I'll come out."

"But—" Fred was talking to a dead line. "Dammit. Good thing you're here, Jonas. I'm going to need you to distract—"

"Good morning, Little Rika."

"Hey, Fred."

"Howdy, fellas." She pulled Jonas to the side so the men could board the ship. "I'll be right there."

She turned to Jonas. "Okay, now it's really good that you're not coming."

Jonas shrugged. "Who cares?"

"Jonas, whoever the bimbo is, forget about her! She's obviously a moron of the highest order and you're way too good for her. So put the bitch out of your mind and focus on me now, please."

"Oh, it's Fred time. Must be Tuesday. Or one of the other six days of the week."

"Sarcasm does not become you," she said stiffly. "And furthermore—"

"Hi, Dr. Bimm!"

They looked. Madison was scampering up the ramp, waving. She wore a peach-colored shell (did she have a closet full of them, in all different colors?) and khaki pants that showed her pubic bone.

"My God," Jonas muttered. "I can see her five o'clock shadow."

Madison screeched to a halt in front of them. "Hi, you guys! Are you going out in the ship?"

"Yes."

"Can I come with? I can look for dolphins."

"No."

"Besides," Jonas said kindly, "there aren't any dolphins in—"

"Oh please please? I won't be any trouble, I swear. You won't even know I'm there!"

"That," Fred said, "is a lie."

Madison looked crushed. "Well . . . maybe your friend can keep me company." She batted her long lashes at Jonas. Actually batted her lashes! Fred didn't think women did that anymore.

"Thanks anyway, honey," Jonas said, "but I'm in mourning for my sex life."

"You—oh. *Oh.*" Fred watched while Madison jumped to the conclusion that Jonas was gay. Normally she'd be irritated for her friend and wouldn't hesitate to correct the mistake, but in this case, Madison was doing Jonas a huge favor.

Furthermore, Dr. Barb was here, approaching them rapidly. Jonas had his back to her, but from where she was standing Fred had a perfect view of—a navy blue suit?

She stared. And stared more when Dr. Barb saw

them and dramatically slowed her trot. In fact, she stopped altogether. And if Fred didn't know better, she'd think Dr. Barb was standing like that to . . . pose?

"Holy cow!" Madison peeped. "Dr. Barb got a haircut! And new clothes!"

Jonas's eyes bulged and he whipped around like it was the boogeyman coming up behind him instead of good old Dr. Barb.

"Jeez," Fred said, impressed. "She looks really good. I had no idea she had such a cute figure under those lab coats."

He whipped back around and now he was glaring at her. "Well, if *you've* noticed, it must be a bona fide transformation."

"Easy there, Bitchy McGee. Don't take your bad week out on me. I'm in charge of taking my bad weeks out on you."

Dr. Barb was slowly (?) making her way up the ramp leading to the loading dock. The clipboard she was holding was forgotten, hanging from one hand down by her side. Jonas turned back around to watch her walk up to them.

"Hi . . . Jonas."

"Hi, Barb."

"I, uh, it's nice to see you again."

"You, too. You look beautiful."

Dr. Barb—eh?—blushed.

Blushed?

"It was, um, a little scary to come in today. I'm afraid I've been avoiding you."

"That's okay. I've been avoiding you, too."

Fred turned to Madison. "Go clean out the lobster tanks."

"But this is much more—"

She gave the younger woman a helpful shove, almost knocking her into the bay. "Bye, now."

Meanwhile, Dr. Barb and Jonas were staring into each other's eyes, oblivious of the nauseating picture they presented.

"I'm so sorry I ran out like that. It was all just such a—"

"That's okay," Jonas said, coming to life for the first time all day. "I kind of sprung it on you."

"Oh, no! I shouldn't have reacted the way I did.

I was too silly to realize the enormous compliment you were paying me. I'd—I'd really like to go somewhere *private* and talk about it."

"You—you would?"

Fred, who had been staring back and forth like she was watching a tennis match, broke in. "You would?"

Jonas reached out. Dr. Barb put her small, chubby hand in his. They started walking down the ramp together. Suddenly Dr. Barb turned, waved the clipboard, and said, "Have a nice ride, Dr. Bimm!"

"Have a nice ride? Don't you remember what happened last time? Don't you care about my welfare? And why are you holding hands with my best friend?"

Jonas waved without even turning around. "Bye, Fred."

"Stop that! Stop that immediately! I don't have time for more complications right now! Jonas! Get your hands off my boss! Jonas! Joooonaaaassss!" Then, in a near whimper, "Dr. Barb?"

Luckily, Jonas obeyed, dropped Dr. Barb's hand, and raced back to her. Now that was more like it!

He sure had gone above and beyond in this whole "distract my boss" thing, but now—

"Give me the key card," he hissed.

"What?"

"Thomas's key card! I know he gave you a spare. Hand it over. You guys aren't going to be back for a while, right?"

"I'm not giving you the key card to a hotel room that isn't mine so you can bang my boss!"

"Yes you are," Jonas said. "Or I'll kick your fishy ass right into this harbor. With all the shit."

"Fine, take it." Fred sulkily handed it over. "Unnecessarily complicate my life, see if I care."

"Okay. Bye!" He scampered back down the ramp, toward the woman he'd had a crush on for six years.

"I didn't mean any of it!" Fred shouted, but the lovebirds ignored her.

Stifling the urge to kick something, she stomped the rest of the way up the ramp.

Twenty-eight

§

Captain O'Donnell was not at all happy to see her.

"Get this nautical menace off my ship," he said by way of greeting to Thomas.

"Calm down, O'Donnell. This is official NEA business."

"And my father's," Artur piped up, interrupting his conversation with a dazed-looking first mate.

"Low profile, dumbass," Thomas snarked.

"That goes for you, too, dumbass," Fred said. She

turned back to the captain and gave him her nicest smile. He recoiled. "Now, Captain, all that stuff is behind us, right? I was a completely different person back then . . . ignorant, willful—"

"It was two months ago, Dr. Bimm."

"But we've both aged decades since then in wisdom, haven't we." At his look of disbelief, she added crossly, "Well, *I* have!"

O'Donnell turned to his first mate. "When was the last time we had a VSC?"

Artur sidled over to her. "The king of the ship seems agitated."

"It's a long story, Artur."

"What is a VSC?"

"Vessel Safety Check."

The first mate checked a chart and said helpfully, "Two weeks ago yesterday, Cap'n."

"Hmm. I *guess* that might be all right." He shot Fred a distrustful look. "Possibly."

Now Thomas was on her left. "Why is the crew treating you like you've brought the plague on board?"

Fred waved away his concern. "A silly misunder-standing that led to, uh, the sinking of his last boat." At Thomas's incredulous stare, she added, "But this one is much nicer than the *Fiona*. Bigger, prettier. Insurance paid for the whole thing, too."

"Dr. Bimm." O'Donnell had approached her carefully, like she was a rattlesnake. "Please go over there. Sit in that chair. Do not move from that chair until you need to throw up. Those are the circumstances that will allow me to overlook the fact that your name was nowhere on my paperwork for today's runs."

"No problem at all, Captain!" she said with a heartiness she didn't feel. She was getting off lightly, and she knew it. He had the power to order anyone—even Dr. Barb—off his ship.

"Little Rika, what did you do?"

"A trifle. I swear!" She started to head to the chair, tripped over a coil of rope, and went sprawling. She would have skinned her nose on the deck if Artur hadn't moved like lightning and caught her. "Uh, I hate to trouble you, but if you could carry me over to my assigned chair?"

"It would be my pleasure, Rika." He set her down in the chair from which she wouldn't move until the puking started. "There you are."

"Thanks." To Thomas: "Stop staring and close your mouth."

"But—you're a marine biologist."

"I'm aware, Thomas."

"But we're only in the harbor."

"I'm *aware*, Thomas!" She leaned over the railing and tossed the rest of her breakfast into the waves.

"Little Rika, how is it that you're ill?"

"Seasick," she groaned, and threw up again. Oh, this was just lovely. Just perfect. Two guys had weird crushes on her and she was sexily throwing up.

"But," Thomas was hissing in her ear, "you're a mermaid!"

"I. Am. Aware. Now get away from me unless you want some on your shoes."

Thomas didn't back away. Instead he leaned on the rail beside her and rubbed her back. "Why didn't you take any Dramamine?"

"Because I metabolize it too quickly. I'd have to take forty for it to work and even then I don't know if—urrgghh."

"Fascinating. And disgusting," he added.

Now there were two hands rubbing her back. "Little Rika, perhaps we should go back and do this tomorrow when you are not ill."

"She's not coming back tomorrow!" Captain O'Donnell yelled from his cabin, where he and the first mate were frantically counting life jackets, flame arresters and visual distress signals.

"Not even if you paid me a million bucks," she snapped back. Then, quietly, "It's no good, Artur. The same thing would happen tomorrow."

"Uh—how are you two going to get in with me without these guys seeing it?" Thomas said.

"Trust me, O'Donnell will be thrilled to see me dive off his ship. As long as I stay out of his way, he could care less what Artur and I are doing."

"You're kidding. He's a maniac about boat safety, but he won't care if you—"

"He's a maniac about boat safety. Not passenger safety. Trust me."

Thomas shook his head and went to put on his scuba suit.

Twenty-nine

🐚

They had narrowed down the suspects to the new seafood restaurant ("Cap'n Clammys!"), the new Sleepytime Hotel and the old (but recently massively renovated) World Trade Center. The plan was for the three of them to dive in, check out the underwater sites, pipes and other detritus of construction, and see if they could pinpoint the bad guy. What they would do then, even if they could find a pipe pouring shit from one building, Fred wasn't sure.

Artur favored strangling the owner until his neck

cracked. Thomas leaned toward ratting them out to the EPA. Fred was torn. Surely the culprit, whoever it was, knew what he (or she) was doing. So there should be a greater consequence than a fine. But neither did she favor murder (though Artur claimed it would be a simple case of self-defense).

Talk about putting the cart before the horse, she thought, diving in beside Artur as Thomas went, in the scuba-approved fashion, over backward. *First we gotta find the guy. (Or gal.) Right now, I'd settle for that.*

Instantly her uneasy stomach settled and she felt loads better. She playfully gave Thomas a pinch (which he probably couldn't feel through all the rubber) and darted past both men.

Feeling better, Little Rika?

Thomas was giving her a cautious thumbs-up.

Loads. Don't use your telepathy to exclude Thomas. She gave him the thumbs-up back.

Do not use my what to do what?

Never mind. Keep your eyes open. And your nose.

I confess I do not know how to feel. I have no urge to taste that particular taste again.

Right there with you, Artur. Oh, look at this.

Thomas was gesturing them over, shining his undersea light at what she assumed was Cap'n Clammy's from below.

Let's get to it.

Ah, Little Rika, your devotion to duty is commendable.

Yeah, that's what they keep telling me.

Thirty

It was difficult to work the key card when Barb had already yanked his pants halfway down to his knees, but Jonas managed. They staggered into the Presidential Suite, struggling with each other's clothes, kissing, panting, groaning, gasping. Jonas tripped over a divan and down they went.

"Ooof!"

"I'm so sorry!" Barb cried, leaning over him. "Are you all right? Am I too heavy? I'll get off."

"Not until I do," he growled, and yanked her

down for another scorching kiss. He heard the thud as one of her pumps hit the carpet (the other one, he was pretty sure, had been abandoned by the door). He undid the one button on her Givenchy jacket and saw the Victoria's Secret matching navy bra beneath.

"Don't you think—" Gasp, moan. "—that this is—" Groan, kiss. "—much better than—" Slobber, sigh. "—lab coats?"

"I'm not giving them up. I just might stop buttoning them all the way." She was straddling him, tugging at his belt, when suddenly she went over as well. Now she was the one groaning, "Ooof!" and he was on top.

Not that he minded being on top.

"Fuck this," he laughed. "Let's go to the bedroom."

"A place this big must have one," she agreed, and he stood and pulled her to her feet.

In the ridiculously opulent bedroom, he carefully pulled off every item of clothing that he had so carefully picked out. She was considerably less careful; at least two of his shirt buttons were gone and he was afraid she had thrown his belt in the garbage.

"I've been thinking about what you said." Tug, tear. "For three days, I've been kicking myself for being such a fool." Yank, pull. "I had a perfect opportunity and I ran away like a ninny." Jerk, rip.

"I've been hiding in my apartment for three days," he said, pushing her back on the bed. "That's not much better. I just wasn't up to facing you after what happened."

"Yes, but that's my fault."

"Well, like I said, I kind of sprung it on you."

"Yes, but like I said, I—"

"Barb?"

"Yes?"

"I'm about to live the six year fantasy. Can we stop talking for, um, ten minutes?"

She grinned up at him. "Ten? Oh, dear."

"Look, it's been a while."

"I'll try to stifle my humiliating laughter."

"That'd be great." He kissed her mouth, her lush, ripe mouth, savoring it so he could replay the moment over and over later, in his lonely bachelor's bed. He kissed her neck as her fingers ran through his hair (thank God Fred had bullied him into a shower!), as she caressed and stroked.

He tugged the cups of her bra down, exposing large creamy breasts and pink nipples that hardened when he stroked them gently. She gasped when he leaned down and sucked one into his mouth.

"Oh my God—Jonas—it's been years since—don't stop."

"Like I could if I wanted to." He kissed her cleavage, stroked one breast while he lavished attention on the other one, and while he was doing that she was yanking at her bra and wriggling out of her underwear.

She rolled over until she was on top, and jerked and pulled at his shorts until they were on the floor. She looked over her shoulder and stared with some satisfaction at his hard-on.

"This is no time for a cutting remark," he warned her.

"In no way was I thinking of one. I was thinking about how men can be beautiful, too."

If possible, he got harder. Definitely the boner of a lifetime. A one-of-a-kind boner, never to be repeated. Yep, there was no topping *this* bone, no way in hell.

"Now fuck me," Barb growled in her school-teacher voice. "Right *now*."

He was wrong! And never so thankful for it. He watched in admiration and lust as she straddled his hips with hers, as she seized him firmly in her hot little hand and guided him inside her. She was more than ready for him and he slid all the way in without the smallest bit of resistance.

"That's better," she said cheerfully, and began riding him like a cowgirl. All she needed was the twirling rope.

He grabbed her hips and surged against her on the downstroke, thinking *I'm going to die I'm going to die she's killing me and thank God thank God . . .*

"Oh, Jonas, that's *wonderful*! Don't stop!" Bounce, bounce.

"I thought you weren't going to talk for ten minutes." He groaned while she slid up and down with exquisite strokes, while her breasts bobbed before him, begging to be kissed, while her mouth curved into a smile and her eyes sparkled.

"I never agreed to that," she said primly, which was a riot given what they were doing.

"I s'pose that's fair." He felt the familiar rumbling in his balls that meant the festivities would soon be over—he hadn't gotten off so quickly with a woman since college. He reached and found Barb's clit and stroked it gently, barely touching it, then more firmly on the downstroke, until she was riding his fingers as she was riding his cock, and then she shivered all over, leaned back, and shrieked at the ceiling.

His fingers whitened on her hips as he felt the rumbling start in his balls and race through his body until he thought the top of his head was going to come off. The room actually tilted one way and then the other as he desperately tried to focus, as Barb collapsed over him with a groan, as the greatest orgasm of his life tore through him like a—those things Fred talked about—

Don't think about Fred, idiot.

Tsunami. Like a tsunami, that was it.

"Oh my," Barb gasped in his ear.

"You're my tsunami."

She sat up and stared down at him thoughtfully, face and breasts flushed from their exertion. "We'll work on the pet names," she said at last, and he tickled her until she begged for mercy.

Thirty-one

"Well, that was a huge waste of time." Fred grumbled, tripping over an ice chest but righting herself in time. The captain helped her onto the ramp and she stomped down it. "Not to mention breakfast."

"We'll keep trying," Thomas said, white-faced with exhaustion. They had been in the water for hours. Fred was sort of ready for a nap herself.

"Perhaps I will go back later, now that I know the locations under suspicion." Artur, annoyingly, looked like he'd just jumped out of bed after fourteen hours of sleep. Stupid full-blooded mermen.

Fred yawned. "Now who's got a commendable devotion to duty?"

"I do not wish to cause you more distress—which the trip on the boat seemed to. And although he annoys me sometimes—I do not wish to see harm come to this one." He pointed to Thomas. "It would not be honorable."

"Yeah, okay, whatever."

"Whatever is right," said Thomas. "I'm going back to the room so I can fall on my face and die for a few hours."

"The room?" Fred halted midway down the ramp. Behind her, the first mate groaned. She flapped a hand at him in a "don't worry" motion and reached for her cell phone. "The room. Right. Let me just see if Jonas wants to come. I mean join us."

"Join us taking a nap?"

"Just let me call him. Right now."

* * *

Barb was cuddling into his side and all was right with the world. "I swear," she murmured, "I haven't had that much fun since my divorce. Actually, since about a year before my divorce."

Jonas yawned. "Right . . . didn't you say he was cheating on you the whole last year?"

"Mm-hmm."

"Dumbass."

"Mm-hmm."

"Not that I'm complaining, but I can't believe someone didn't swoop down on you after you got rid of the idiot."

She giggled. "Someone did. It just took them a few years to get their act together."

"Off my case. Keeping Fred out of trouble is a full-time job, and I already *have* one of those."

She was tracing circles around his left nipple, which his entire body thought was fine. "That's my ex, too. He's always taking on new projects, extra jobs. He built a hotel just a couple blocks away from here—would you believe he had the nerve to send me an invitation to the grand opening last month?"

"Should have told him to stick it where the sun never ever shines." He ruffled her newly short hair—shoulder length, layered around the face. Just as he had suggested. "I love your hair like this. God, it's like silk, it's—your husband did what?"

Barb's eyes were closed as she luxuriated in his touch, but now they popped open. "I didn't quite catch that."

He could hardly hear her. He was trying hard to remember what Fred had said about their little harbor problem. Literal shit into the water. Likely from a new building. One built in the last year. And then there was the personal angle, something he bet neither Thomas nor the prince had considered.

What if someone was fucking up Boston Harbor to wreck things for the NEA? Tough to get tourists down to Shitville. Tough to do much of anything when the entire harbor smelled like a Porta Potti.

"Your ex. What's his name?"

"Phillip King."

"So you've always had your own name."

"Jonas, what's the matter?"

He ignored the question. "Think this one over before you answer, Barb. Did you guys really part amicably?"

"Yes. Although—it's quite funny you should bring this up, because a year ago he started trying to, I guess woo me would be the word. But I wasn't going down that road again, and I told him so. There were some pretty hard feelings that time, and he left a few nasty messages on my machine, but I had my lawyer tell him to cease and desist and that was really the end of—Jonas, what's the matter? You look like you're going to faint."

He could hear his cell phone ringing from somewhere and sat up, gently pushing Barb away. "Help me find my pants," he said urgently.

"But what's the—"

"My pants, woman!"

She hopped off the bed and they both looked in the bedroom and the sitting area. On the third ring he found them hanging from the front doorknob. He lunged for them, found his phone, fumbled with it, dropped it, bent, picked it up, clawed it open.

"Fred, don't hang up!"

"That's not your midorgasm voice, is it?"

He slid to the floor, relieved. "No, but I did just give your boss the banging of a lifetime."

"Oh, Jonas!" she shrieked. "Stop that! I have to work with the woman, you know."

"Ow!"

"What? Did you bruise a testicle?"

"No, she pinched me. Guess she didn't care for my confession, either." She went in for another pinch and he batted her away. "Listen, you guys have any luck?"

"No we did not, dammit, and everybody is pooped—except the King of the Ocean, here, who looks ready to take on the Chicago Bulls—so we're all coming back to the room for a nap and you'd by God better be finished and *fully* dressed when we get there, because one more shock my heart *cannot* take and if you had any sensitivity at all you wouldn't have had sex with my boss in the water fellow's—"

"Fred, *shut the hell up and listen, goddammit!*"

Barb, bending over to shake out her skirt, froze.

"Did you have an aneurysm for lunch?" Fred demanded. "Because—"

"Barb's ex-husband is really pissed at her. And he just built a new hotel. Guess where?"

"Oh, no."

"Right on the harbor."

"Oh, fuck."

"Yup."

"Oh, jeez."

"Yeah. Sic 'em."

"You mean we've been up to our eyeballs in paperwork and Artur and I have been breathing shit—literally breathing shit—and all that we needed to do to crack the case was stand back and let you bone my boss?"

He took the skirt from Barb and tossed it on the dining room table. Then he lifted Barb to the same table. "Looks like. Listen, take your time coming back, will you?"

"Oh, that is just disgus—"

He hung up on her.

"What's this about my ex?" Barb asked, leaning

back and stretching out on the table, which was plenty big enough for four more Barbs.

"Oh. That. He's the bad guy."

"Oh. I'll likely be much more concerned about this..." Jonas began to nibble her cleavage. "Later," she sighed.

"Ummmm," he agreed.

Then, after a long moment: "Is Dr. Bimm angry?"

"Only because she didn't get laid. And that's her own damn fault, believe me."

She arched beneath his hands and wrapped her legs around his waist. "That's nice," she sighed, kissing him back.

He came up for air. "Wait, wait! I've always wanted to try this." He went to the small credenza at the other end of the dining room table, opened it, and withdrew a pack of cards.

"Oh, oh," Barb said, but she was smiling.

Jonas shuffled the cards. "Okay, check this. We'll play poker to get our fantasy."

"We'll do what?"

"We're going to role play. If I win, you're a damsel

in distress and I have to save you, blah-blah. If you win, you're a Catholic school teacher and I've just been caught putting a smoke bomb in the boy's room."

Dr. Barb started to laugh, then choked it off and looked grave. "You feel the need to play cards to bring this about?"

"Hey, I'm a traditionalist." He did a fast box shuffle, then dealt them each five cards. He picked up his hand and observed the three aces. "Okay, whatcha got?"

"I have two twos," she said triumphantly.

He tossed his hand down and grabbed her. "You win, teacher."

Thirty-two

🦄

"Are you sure you're not too tired?" Fred asked as the three of them charged into the Sleepytime Hotel. It was a twelve-story building built right up to the harbor. From the outside it looked like a perfectly respectable, almost luxury hotel. Not at all the den of evil they now knew it to be.

"Now? No way. As soon as you told me, I got a massive adrenaline surge. Let's kick some ass and then turn him over to the EPA."

"After we snap his spine," Artur added.

"You just keep your hands to yourself, buster, until we figure out what we're going to—Phillip King, please," she told the receptionist. In a moment that would haunt her nightmares for eternity, she'd blanked out and had to call Jonas back to get the guy's name. And her friend was so out of breath he could hardly spit it out. And there was an odd thumping noise in the background—not like they were on a bed, but maybe—

"Remind me not to eat anywhere in your suite until I figure this out," she muttered, shrugging when Thomas gave her a mystified look.

"I'm sorry," the receptionist said, "but Mr. King is in a meeting right now and can't be—"

"Tell him," she said, "it's about his ex-wife. I bet he'll see us."

"I bet he will, too," the receptionist muttered. Then she pushed a couple of buttons on her console, gestured to the elevator, and said, more graciously, "Top floor."

"Remember," Fred said as they marched into the elevator, "nobody use the bathrooms while we're here."

"Oh, Fred, that's gross!"

"Just sayin'. Artur, what the hell's the matter with you?" For he had suddenly thrown himself against her and was clutching her hard enough to hurt.

"This little metal box—moving—up?"

"Yeah, it's an elevator, it's perfectly normal, now leggo." She tried to pry his fingers off her arm. "Artur, calm down."

"But what is to prevent the box from shooting right out of the top of the building?"

"Nothing," Thomas said cheerfully. "Happens at least once a week in this city."

"Owwwww," Fred bitched. "Artur, you're cutting off the *circulation*. Thomas, cut the shit."

"I just think he should prepare himself."

"Owwwww!"

There was a *ding* and then the elevator slowed to a stop and the doors hummed open. Artur lost no time in getting out. Thomas went sailing after him, thanks to Fred's helpful shove. He stumbled into Artur, sending them both sprawling in the hallway.

"I swear, the trouble you two cause me on a

minute-by-minute basis . . ." She stomped past them and resisted the urge to kick Thomas in the ribs. At least they were helping each other up like gentlemen.

"You have to admit, I gotcha good," Thomas said.

"Indeed you did. I shall remember your deviousness and address it another time."

"Bring it, you redheaded overgrown—"

"Dr. Bimm, Dr. Pearson and Prince Artur of the Black Sea," Fred announced, walking into the conference room the receptionist had directed them to. Artur had made it clear he wanted his true name and affiliation known when they finally confronted the bad guy.

Bad *guys*.

Fourteen men were staring back at her, and they were all shifty-eyed and shiny-suited, and wore suspicious bulges under their armpits—even the guy at the head of the table, a balding, cadaverously thin man with eyes the color of dust and the longest fingers she'd ever seen. And her mom taught piano.

Of course, on their date, he hadn't been packing. But otherwise she recognized him immediately.

"You said this was about my ex?" Phillip King asked, standing at the head of the table.

"No, it's about what you're *doing* to your ex. Specifically, pumping all the shit from your hotel into her harbor. Well, Boston Harbor. But we know why you're doing it."

That ought to fix him, she thought, folding her bony arms across her chest. And right in front of his partners, too!

One of the shiny-suited men looked at King and said, "I thought you said there was no way to get caught."

"Uh," Fred said. "What?"

"There wasn't," King said, looking startled.

"I thought you said it'd be cheaper to just dump the stuff straight to the harbor—"

"It *is*."

"—and nobody'd be able to tell it was us."

"They can't!"

That's true, Fred thought. They didn't have any hard evidence yet. Which might be problematic.

"Before you get any wise ideas," she added, suddenly *very* glad there were two men on her side, and they were Thomas and Artur, "we told at least a dozen people about this today before we came over here."

"Your hair is still wet," King observed.

"Yeah, but—" She cast about for a convincing lie.

"Miscreant! You admit your wrongdoing? Then be prepared to pay the penalty!"

Which Artur completely ruined.

"You guys are way too mob chic," Thomas said, staring at the men. "Don't even tell me you got laundered crime money to help you build the hotel."

"Of course I did," King snapped. "Where else would I have been able to raise the money so fast? Get the building up so quickly? Get around certain pesky rules and regulations on waste treatment?"

"He's only telling us this," Fred explained to Artur, "because he's going to try to kill us. Just so you know."

"Is that a custom in your world? Talking, then killing?"

"Yeah, I'd say so—Thomas?"

Thomas nodded. "That's the way we bipeds do it."

"You three, go wait in my office. I want to hear more about my ex. And you guys—wait!" For all the other men were standing, getting coats, grabbing suitcases and generally making the noise of men about to leave. "There's no need to cut the meeting short. I've got charts that show just how profitable a whole Sleepytime chain could be and there's no reason why we can't—"

"A chain?" Fred gasped, horrified.

"We'll see how you handle this problem first," one of the shiny-suited men told him. "Then we'll be back. Maybe."

Fred watched with relief as the mobsters left. She had no desire to explain to Artur about gunfights. Or organized crime.

Phillip King opened the door connecting one room to the other and disappeared.

"I guess he's going to his office," Thomas said.

"Then let us meet him on his own territory," Artur announced, striding after him.

"Oh, yeah, I'm sure he just wants to chat," Fred muttered, following the men. Still, King was just one guy—a biped, as Artur would say—and there were three of them. She wasn't especially worried now.

She walked into a brightly lit office with blueprints plastered on every wall (no doubt plans for the mighty Sleepytime empire) and looked at King just in time to see him point something shiny at them.

"Down!" Thomas shouted, and batted her sideways so hard, she flew back into the conference room. At the same instant, or so it felt to her, there was a loud *bang* and a chunk of wood where her head had just been leapt from the wall and fell on the carpet.

Thomas shoved her under the table, yanked Artur down, and in a few seconds all three of them were crouched beneath the conference room table while King screamed things like, "I'm turning that whore's water zoo into a shit hole!" and "It's her fault I'm in debt up to my eyeballs!" and "Why couldn't she just look the other way like a normal wife?" Each rant, of course, punctuated with a gunshot.

"Uh . . ."

"He's nuts," Thomas said, squinting up from beneath the table. "And that is my professional opinion as a water fellow."

Her phone rang and, out of pure dumb habit, she flipped it open. "Yeah?"

"Call the cops on that thing!" Thomas hissed.

"You bipeds and your odd loud weapons."

"It's possible," came Jonas's pant, sounding like he'd just run the two hundred, "that her ex is emotionally disturbed."

"*Now* you tell me. Say, could you send the police to his hotel, if it's not too much trouble?"

"Why? What'd you do to him?"

"Nothing! Except possibly disrupt his illegal funding. But seeing as how he's *shooting* at us, *maybe* you could finish *boinking* my *boss* and *call* some *authorities*." She slapped the phone shut. "Jonas is calling the cavalry. I think. Now what?"

"Well. It looked like a revolver to me. Six shots. I've counted four so far."

"Super. A water fellow who knows about guns." To Artur, "That means he has two left."

"Two what?"

"Two small pieces of metal which his weapon will hurl at us so fast, if it hits a vital organ it will kill us."

Artur made a face. "A distasteful way to fight."

"Hey, let's talk him into stopping, I'm all for it. Any actual ideas?"

"We hope he fires off two more shots in his hysteria, which, if they're anything like the last four, won't come near us. We wait for the police and let them deal with it." Thomas was ticking their options off on his fingers. "Or we goad him into using his last shots. Or we try to take the gun away from him."

"Cowering in terror while we hope he wastes his last two sounds good to me," Fred said.

"Or you could goad him while Artur and I try to sneak in through the other door and jump him."

"Naw."

"Yes," Artur said. "You excel at goading. And hiding does not befit royalty. Come, Thomas."

"Wait a minute!" Fred hissed. But they were already crawling to the other end of the table and slipping out the door. "Dammit!"

She thought for a second. Then took a breath and

yelled, "Hey, King! Did I mention your ex is fucking my best friend?"

Long silence, followed by, "That's a lie. Barb's frigid. She hates sex."

"Sex with *you*, maybe. Either that or my friend cured her because brother, she's already done it twice today. And it's not even . . ." She looked at her watch. "Three o'clock! Guess she's not missing you too much, huh?"

"Who's your friend?"

Fred wasn't sure which was scarier: when he was out of control and firing a gun at random people he'd just met, or when he was scarily calm and trying to think his way out of a hole.

"Put the gun down and maybe I'll tell you. Heck, put the gun down and I'll bring you to him. Them. Did I mention my friend—his dick is about a foot long, according to legend—gave Dr. Barb a makeover? She looks awesome. Did you know that dark blue is her color?"

"White is her color! She buttons her lab coats all the way to the top!"

"Not today, pal. Today I bet she doesn't even know where her lab coat *is*. You know how it is, young love and all that . . ."

King snorted. "My ex is a lot of things, but young isn't one of them."

Gotcha. "Well, maybe, but that doesn't bother my friend. He loves older women. Literally! As in, I'm pretty sure he's loving one right now. She's got to have fifteen years on him."

"She's fucking . . . a younger guy?"

"Multiple times," Fred assured him, no longer having to fake cheerfulness. *This is kind of fun. The guys were right: goading is my gift.* "I hope they're using birth control, because Dr. Barb's not exactly ready for the nursing home yet."

"She's on 'the pill' for her cramps," King replied absently.

"Oh, well, no bouncing babies for her right now. That's okay; with her career, and my friend's career, and all the hot monkey sex they're having, they prob'ly aren't ready for kids."

Silence.

And more silence.

Fred cautiously looked up and saw King framed in the doorway between his office and the conference room. He was pointing the gun straight at her. The barrel, from her standpoint, looked awfully big. She raised her hands and slowly climbed to her feet, thinking, *Damned if I'm going to die on my knees.*

"I'm a big fan of shooting the messenger," he said. "And you're another frigid bitch, if memory serves."

"Why does that not surprise me in the least?" *Come on, guys, what are you waiting for?*

As if in answer to her prayers, the other office door splintered down the middle. But King didn't look around. He didn't even jump. Instead, he shot Fred with his last two bullets.

Thirty-three

There were three things Fred would never forget from that afternoon.

Number one: when you're shot, you don't stagger dramatically backward or plunge out the eleventh-story window. You just stand there.

Number two: Artur can break a man's neck with one effortless twist, and it sounds like the sound ice makes when you crunch it between your teeth.

And number three: Thomas carried a switchblade.

"Uh," Fred began, as King's body was falling, as Artur went red with rage, as Thomas was trying to get her to lie down. "I think I'm—uh—shot."

"You are shot, Fred. Twice."

"Why are you pushing me?"

"Because I want you on your back while I'm getting the bullets out."

She removed his hands. "I really don't like the sound of that." She felt she was being calm and reasonable, and didn't understand why Thomas was as pale as Artur was purple. It didn't hurt at all. And the bad guy was dead.

"Artur! That cabinet over there. Bring me one of the bottles with either white or brown liquid in it." Thomas swept his foot beneath hers and knocked her off balance, then knelt on her chest to keep her on the floor.

There was the sound of glass breaking, and then Artur was kneeling beside her. "Will these assist you, Dr. Pearson?"

That's the first time Artur's called him Doctor.

"Hey, wait a minute!" Fred yelled, wriggling beneath his knee. "He's not a *real* doctor! I mean, he is, but he's not a medical doctor. He's a water fellow."

"I got my M.D. before I went back for my Ph.D. I just found out I had zero interest in triple shifts and other benefits of residency. I don't like working *too* hard to save people's lives."

"You sound like a real winner, Doc."

"Fred, you're never sick. And you said you have an incredibly fast metabolism. So I'm betting your bullet wounds will be all healed over tomorrow." He wiped his blade on the carpet, and then on his pants.

Artur was kneeling beside them and, at some odd prearranged signal she must have missed, suddenly tore her shirt straight down the middle.

"Hey!"

Thomas ignored her. "So we can leave the bullets in you, which would be bad, or we can take you to a hospital for removal, where they'll do all sorts of tests, which would be bad. Or I can take them out right here before they heal over." He unscrewed a bottle of Jack

Daniels, thumbed the button on his switchblade and poured booze all over the knife and his hands.

"But—"

"Hold her down," Thomas said shortly, and went to work.

Thirty-four

Jonas and Barb were sitting at the bar in the Presidential Suite, drinking wine (eh, Thomas was rich, he could afford a bottle of Chardonnay) and having a perfectly nice chat about how they planned to spend the rest of their lives together, when the front door rattled.

"Fortunately we're fully clothed," Barb teased. "Finally."

"I still say we should have gone over to your ex's hotel and caught the ruckus. I mean, there were a million sirens a while ago. I bet it was cool."

Barb shook her head. "If the police require a statement of course I'll cooperate. But best to leave things to the professionals."

Fred stomped in, looking like somebody had worked her over pretty good. Jonas was off the stool and on his feet before he was aware he'd moved. She'd been his sparring partner more than once, and taken full kicks in the face without so much as a bruise. But now Fred was wearing a blood-stained bra and her favorite (and now also bloody) pair of track shorts. And how many times did he have to beg her not to wear tennis shoes without socks? Yech.

Thomas and Artur came in behind her and they looked almost as bad: both of them spattered with blood

(whose blood?????)

and Thomas sporting what was going to be one hell of a black eye, and Artur with a split lip.

"Little Rika, surely you could see Dr. Pearson knew what he was—"

"Fred, come on, don't be mad. I did it to save you from—"

"I said *no* talking to me *ever*!" Fred whirled on Barb. "And you! Your crazy ex husband *shot* me. Twice! Also, he's dead."

Barb's mouth hung ajar. "What? Phillip is dead?"

"And he *shot* me."

"But you never get hurt," Jonas managed.

"Well, if someone points a big gun at me and pulls the fucking trigger, I can get hurt, okay, genius? Luckily, Dr. Demento and his faithful lab wretch, Artur the Psycho, were there to save the day. And by save the day, I mean commit federal fucking assault!" Fred kicked the leg of the eight-foot dining room table. Said leg collapsed like it was a toothpick, and there was a tremendous *whud* as the thing crashed to the floor.

"And you two! Boning the afternoon away while we're cleaning up the shit your ex left behind! Him and the *Mafia*. Thanks for nothing!"

"Phillip has ties to the *Mafia*?" Barb gasped.

"Had, Dr. Barb. He's dead."

"We did call the police and send them over," Jonas

said weakly. "How could we have known a matter for the EPA was going to turn into a Mafia-laden bloodbath?"

"On the same day both of you get laid for the first time in years? You didn't think that was a sign of the Apocalypse? Because I sure as shit did! You two can't have sex again, ever."

Jonas and Barb looked at each other, then at Fred. "You mean ever ever? Or just with each other?"

"I think, to be on the safe side—" Fred stopped in midrant and put a shaking hand to her forehead. Artur and Thomas quietly walked up until they were each standing just behind her. "I think—I think you better not—ever—"

Then the oddest thing of the entire afternoon (and it had been a doozy) happened: Fred's eyes rolled up until Jonas could only see the whites, and she pitched backward.

Thomas and Artur caught her, neat as you please, and Artur lifted her up and laid her on the couch.

"Is there any more of that wine left?" Thomas

asked, once he had made sure Fred would be fine. He touched his swelling eye and winced. "It's been a helluva day."

"If that is a drink like ale or grog, I also would like some." Artur's split lip was also swelling nicely.

Barb poured. They clinked. They drank. Fred snored.

Thirty-five

Fred rolled over, felt a stabbing pain in her shoulder, grabbed it and groaned. Grabbing it made it worse, so she opened her eyes.

She was on the couch in the living room of the Presidential Suite. And it was dark out.

"Wakey wakey," Thomas said. He was holding her wrist in one hand and looking at his watch.

She yanked her arm out of his grasp and fought the urge to blacken his other eye. The holding-down bullet-removing game had not been fun. For any of them.

"What's going on? Where is everybody?"

"Barb and Jonas are down at the police station giving their statements. Artur is conked out in the bedroom."

"I'm not speaking to you," she said coldly, "but if I was, I would wonder how you explained King's neck being broken by a merman."

"We don't know anything about that. We didn't see what happened. Maybe he slipped. Maybe one of his mob buddies came back and paid a visit. All we know is that he tried to kill a couple of people, we ran away, and he violated about a thousand EPA regs. He's dead, so I don't give a shit. Let the cops and the bureaucrats sort it out."

Thomas sounded pretty cold during his little speech, and Fred suppressed a shiver. "What are you so mad about? Which is what I would ask if I were speaking to you. Which I am not."

He had leaned in to look at her pupils, but suddenly his gaze shifted and he was seeing her, not her eyes. "Fred, he shot you! If Artur hadn't broken his neck, I would have stuck my knife into more than his kidney. He just stood there and shot you. And then I had to dig my knife into your shoulder while Artur held you down and you screamed the place down and cried and begged me—God!" He ran shaking hands through his dark hair, making it stand up in wild clumps. "For putting all of us through that, I could kill him right now all over again."

"Well, all right, calm down. It's no big deal. It's all over. Bad guy's dead. We win. Drinks all around." She started to sit up, grimacing. "I'd kill for an aspirin to work, there's no doubt about—oof!"

Thomas had put a hand on her chest and slammed her back down. "You *stay down*," he said.

"Don't push your luck," she warned him.

"Stay," he said again. "Do not make me get Artur in here to make you lie down, Fred. You won't like it and neither will I." He got up and started to pace, looking like he was going to leap out of his skin.

She watched him, amazed. "Thomas, what in the world's gotten into you?"

He whirled on her, dark eyes flashing. "What's gotten *into* me?"

"Well, yeah, that's kind of where I was going with my whole 'what's gotten into you' question."

"How about this? I love you, you silly bitch, and thanks to that fucker King I had to hurt you. Not exactly all part of my plan for a romantic goddamned evening!"

"But—you—but you don't even—we haven't even known each other a week!"

He plunked down in the chair opposite her and waved away her objection. "Oh, hell with that. I knew the minute I saw you in the tank. Of course I love you. How could I love anybody but you?"

"But you're only going to be here for a couple of weeks! Then it's off to Millport!" Millport was the University Marine Biology Station in Scotland.

He smiled at her, but oh, such a tired, bitter grin. She almost wished he hadn't smiled at all. "Been checking on my schedule, huh? And it's sooner than that, babe. My project here is finished."

"Well. I wasn't sure how long our shit project was going to take, that's why I checked your schedule."

He propped his hand on his chin and looked at her

for a long moment. Finally, he said, "Go back to sleep. I'm sorry I dumped all that on you. I should have waited until you were feeling better."

"You shouldn't have dumped it on me at all."

Thomas shrugged. "Better get used to hearing it. If I have to think it, you have to hear it."

Fred, having never been in love before, said crossly, "I don't think that's how it goes."

"Go back to sleep."

"I'm not tired."

"Yes you are. You lost a ton of blood in the conference room. You almost ended up in the hospital despite my best efforts."

"Well. Thanks for that."

"Finally, a glimmer of gratitude. I may faint."

"Shut up, I'm still not speaking to you."

"I know."

"And I'm not tired," she said, and while they were arguing about it, she fell asleep.

Thirty-six

🐚

"Rika?"

A hand on her, shaking her. Time for school already? Wasn't it Saturday?

"Rika?"

"Five more minutes," she groaned.

"Little Rika, I will be gone in three."

That was not Moon Bimm. That was—

She opened her eyes. Artur was on his knees beside the couch. He was so close that strands of his red hair were tickling her face.

"Gone in three?" Why did her brain feel like it had turned to oatmeal? Why was she so tired? Where was everybody? "Why? Where is everybody?"

"Your supervisor and your friend went back to your friend's domicile many hours ago. Thomas is resting. And I must leave. The king requires a full report."

"*Leaving* leaving? Leaving right now?"

"The king calls and I must answer. But I could not leave without seeing how you are. I do profoundly apologize for violating your boundaries—"

"What?"

"Holding you down," he translated. "But I felt Thomas was right. It was best to remove the metal things from your body. Metal does not belong in bodies. However, doing so against your will was—" He looked away. "Difficult."

"Oh, yeah. I can see how that must have been so difficult. For *you two*." She rubbed her shoulder, which still ached. "Lucky for me I'm not prone to infections."

"Rika, when you are strong once again, I will return."

"Why?"

"Because you are my princess meant," he replied simply.

"What?"

"My—fiancée? Except you have not given me your hand so we are only promised to be promised."

"Artur—*what*?"

"You will be the Princess of the Black Sea," he told her, completely ignoring her shushing motions, "and one day you and I will be the High King and Queen after my dear father is gone."

"No. We. Won't!"

He smiled at her. "Ah, yes. Biped wooing. Thomas warned me."

"*Thomas* warned you?"

"Yes, it is an odd thing, being fond of my greatest rival, but I cannot help it. He is decisive, clever, duplicitous and violent. All the things that make the bipeds formidable. He informed me that you will be his and not mine, but we have agreed to woo you in our own ways and ultimately let you make the choice when you are ready."

"But—but—but—"

"He will lose, of course. And now, I go."

Artur got to his feet without using his hands, which looked impressive, and strode to the door. She sat up, swung her legs off the couch, ignored the shooting pains and raced after him.

"You can't just leave!"

"But I must."

"But you can't just say all that—that *stuff* and then just march out the door!" *Not both of them,* she thought frantically. *Not* both *of them!*

"But I will come back." He cupped the back of her neck, kissed her sweetly, then opened the door. "I will always come back."

He closed the door with a soft click.

"But I don't want to be the High Queen of the Black Sea!" she shouted at the closed door.

"What are you doing out of bed?" Thomas asked sleepily, standing in the bedroom doorway.

"It's not a bed, it's a couch. And who could go to sleep right now?"

He yawned. "Did Artur leave? God, finally. He's not bad, for an arrogant, entitled, overbearing, non-intellecutal, pompous . . ." There was more in this vein, but Fred didn't catch it, as Thomas had turned around and gone back to bed.

The doorknob rattled and she stared at it fearfully. What was that line from Dorothy Parker? Or was it Shakespeare? "What fresh hell is this?" From Hamlet or some damned thing, and that's just how she felt, too, like some fresh hell was lurking around the—

She yanked the door open. Barb and Jonas were in a clinch, from which they separated with difficulty.

"You two," she said bitterly, and went back inside. She fished a bottle of water from the wet bar (what the hell, Thomas could afford it) and ignored the cooing, cuddling couple behind her.

"Feeling better?" Jonas asked with grating cheer. "Because, girlfriend, you look like shit on a plate."

"Thank you so much," she replied, taking a deep swig. "Not all of us could spend the afternoon mating like rabbits. And what are you doing here, anyway?"

"It's 7:00 a.m.," Jonas pointed out. "Barb wanted to get an early start at the NEA since she played hooky yesterday, and I figured I'd check on you and give you a ride home if you wanted. Oh, and give you a shirt. Seeing as how your last one—"

"Don't remind me. Artur left."

"Yeah, we saw him in the hall, but he's coming back pretty soon."

"And Thomas has to go to Scotland."

"Yes, I imagine now that he's solved his toxin problem, he'll be leaving sooner rather than later," Dr. Barb said. "I'd better get started on the paperwork."

"They're both in love with me. I mean, they said they were."

"Well, duh," Jonas snarked.

"Of course they are," Dr. Barb said. "Didn't you know?"

Fred glared at her boss and her best friend. "What am I going to *do*?"

"Heal up," Jonas suggested.

"Yes, get well soon," Dr. Barb replied. Two peas in a pod, these two. That wasn't going to get old fast, oh heavens no. "I suspect you will need all of your strength in the coming weeks."

Jonas winked at her when Barb couldn't see. Well. At least she had *some* secrets left. And Dr. Barb was sure right about needing her strength. Because if this is the stuff that happened to her when men were in love, she shuddered to think of the engagement.

Not that she was going to get engaged. To either of those yo-yos. But if she were, she would definitely pick . . .

Er . . .

Well, for *sure* she'd pick . . . ah . . .

Oh dear, she thought glumly, and downed the rest of the water in three gulps.

Turn the page for a special preview of
MaryJanice Davidson's new novel

Undead and Uneasy

Coming soon from Berkley Sensation!

A Letter to My Readers:

First of all, thank you, dear reader. It's standard to refer to you as "dear" but you really are dear to me, and I'll tell you why. Thanks to you, I've gone from the excitement of never knowing when the power will be shut off (during a party? when my folks are over? during my kid's science experiment?) to the staid, dull lifestyle of one who can actually pay her utility bills. Because of my readers, I never go to a book signing unless I'm sporting a) designer shoes or b) a pedicure. Because of my readers, I've gotten to research mermaids, ghosts, psychics, manta rays, the Caymans, Florida, Cape Cod, Monterey Bay, Texas, zombies (Texas zombies?), vampires, were-anythings, Alaska, royal lineage, Martha Stewart, bellinis vs. mimosas, bed and breakfasts, wax fangs, and why nobody starts smoking at age thirty-five.

I've also learned how to write an ongoing series versus a stand-alone single-title novel.

Which brings us to *Undead and Uneasy*.

If you've been with me since the beginning, since *Undead and Unwed*, bless you. Your patience is about to be rewarded, I think. If you're new to the series, you've come along just in time: as one of the weird sisters in *Hercules* said, "It's gonna be big."

Everything in the Undead universe has been leading to this book (say it with me: poor Betsy!). Yes, there has been a method to my madness. The support group she has so carefully, if unconsciously, been building around herself—that I've been building for her—is about to disappear. Everything she thought she knew about the undead? Totally wrong. Marriage? Life? Death? It's all, like her favorite book and movie, Gone with the Wind.

That's not to say we won't have some fun along the way . . . Those of you who've been with me before know that the Undead universe is always a good time. It's just . . . we're not all going to make it out alive. And I'm sorry. I know that sucks. But it's just . . . it's just how life is sometimes. And death.

So, dear reader, thank you for coming along for the ride. Thank you for *staying* along for the ride. You won't be sorry, I'm pretty sure. And if you are? Well, I can write fast or I can write long, but I can't do both. This is the long version, so what say we give it a try?

So let's get going, shall we? As Betsy might say, "Pipe down and listen up, asshat."

You are cordially invited to
the wedding of

Elizabeth Anne Taylor

and

Sinclair

607 Summit Avenue
Midnight
July 4, 2007

RSVP by June 25, and don't be like one of those jerks who doesn't RSVP and then shows up with three people. Seriously.

One

~

"There are three things wrong with that card," the king of the vampires told me. "One: my love for you is not as shimmering as amber waves of summer wheat. Two: my love for you has nothing to do with rabbits. Three: rabbits do not sparkle."

I looked at the shiny yellow card, aglitter with sparkling bunnies. It was the least objectionable of the pile of two dozen I had spread all over our bed. What could I say? He had a point. Three of them.

"It's just an example; don't have a heart attack and friggin' die on me, all right?"

"I do not have," he muttered, "that kind of good fortune."

"I heard that, pal. I'm just saying, there will be a lot of people at the wedding"—I ignored Sinclair's shudder—"but there will also be people who can't make it. You know, due to having other plans or being dead or whatever. So what you do is, you send a wedding announcement to all the people who couldn't come. That way people know we actually did the deed. It's polite." I racked my brain for the perfect way to describe it so my reluctant groom would climb on board. "It's, you know, civilized."

"It is a voracious grab for gifts from the crude and uncouth."

"That's true," I acknowledged after a minute, knowing well where I was in the Wars of the Couth. Come on, we all knew he was right. There was no point—*no* point—in all those birth and wedding and graduation announcements beyond "Hey! Limber up the old checkbook; something new has happened in our family. Cash is also fine." "But it's still nice to do. You didn't fuss nearly so much about the invitations."

"The invitations have a logical point."

"The invitations are weird. 'Sinclair,' like you don't have a middle or first name. I'm marrying Cher!"

"Don't tease."

I bit my tongue for what felt like the hundredth time that night . . . and it was barely nine p.m. With the wedding only three weeks away, Sinclair, my blushing groom, was growing bitchier by the hour.

He had never liked the idea of a formal wedding with a minister and flower girls and a wedding cake frosted with colored Crisco. He said that because the Book of the Dead proclaimed him my consort, we were married for a thousand years. Period. End of discussion. Everything else? A waste of his time. And money. Tough to tell the greater sin in his eyes.

After what *seemed* like a thousand years (but was only one and a half) I'd gotten Eric (yes, he had a first name) to profess his love, propose, give me a ring and agree to a ceremony. But he never promised to take his dose without kicking, and he sure never promised to get married without a heavy dose of snark.

I had two choices. I could rise to his bitchy comments with a few of my own and we could end up in a wicked big fight, again. Or, I could ignore his bitchy comments and go about my day, er, night, and after the wedding Sinclair would be my sweet, blushing boytoy again.

Then there was the honeymoon to look forward to: two weeks in New York City, a place I'd never been! I'd heard NYC was a great place to visit, if you had money. Sinclair had gobs. Ew, which reminded me.

"By the way, I'm not taking your name. It's nothing personal—"

"Not personal? It is my name."

"—it's just how I was raised."

"Your mother took your father's name and, even after he left her for the lethal flirtations of another woman, kept his name. Which is why, to this day, there are two Mrs. Taylors in town. In fact, it is *not* how you were raised."

I glared. He glared back, except his was more like a sneer. Since Sinclair looked like he was sneering even when he was unconscious, it was tough to tell. All I knew was, we were headed for yet another argument, and thank goodness we were doing it in our bedroom, where one of the house's many live-ins wasn't likely to bother us. Or, even worse, rate us (Marc had given our last fight a 7.6 but had taken points off for lack of originality in name-calling).

We lived (and presumably would for the next thousand years—hope Jessica was paid up on her damage insurance) in a big old mansion on Summit Avenue in St. Paul. Me, Sinclair, my best friend Jessica, Marc and a whole bunch of others I'm just too tired (or not drunk enough) to list right now. Our room, since there were two of us, was the biggest and the nicest. The master suite. I'd never seen a divine bathroom before, but after taking a bath in the eight-foot-long whirlpool tub, I'd come to believe God could act through bubbles.

The whole place was like a bed and breakfast—the fanciest, nicest one in the whole world, where the fridge was always full, the sheets were always fresh and you never had to check out and go home. Even the closets were sublime, with more scrollwork than you could shake a stick at. Having come from a long line of tract housing–dwellers, I'd resisted the move here last year. But now I loved it. I still couldn't believe I actually lived in a *mansion* of all things, but I loved it. The bedroom was so big, I hardly noticed Sinclair.

Okay, that was a lie. Eric Sinclair filled every room he was in, even if he was just sitting in the corner reading a newspaper. Big—well over six feet—with the build of a farmer (which he had been) who kept in shape (which he did): wide, heavily muscled shoulders, long legs, narrow waist, flat stomach, big hands, big teeth, big dick. Alpha male all the way. And he was mine. Mine, I tell you!

Sinclair was seventy-something—I was vague on the details and he rarely volunteered bio info—but had died in his thirties, so his black hair was unmarked by gray; his broad, handsome face was without so much as a sun wrinkle. He had a grin that made Tom Cruise look like a snaggletoothed octogenarian. He was dynamite in bed—ooh, boy, was he! He was rich (possibly richer than my best friend, Jessica, who was the richest person in the state). He was strong—I'd seen him pull a man's arm off his body like you or I would pull a chicken wing apart. And I mentioned the vampire part, right? That he was the king of the vampires?

And I was the queen. *His* queen.

Never mind what the Book of the Dead said; never mind what other vampires said; shit, never mind what my *mom* said. I loved Eric (when he wasn't being a pud) and he loved me (I was almost positive), and in my book (which wasn't bound in human skin and written in blood, *thank you very much*) that meant we got a justice of the peace to say Husband And Wife. (Two years ago, I would have said a minister. But if a man of God said a blessing over him, sprinkled him with Holy Water or handed him a collection plate, my darling groom would go up in flames and it'd be really awkward.)

Anyway, that was the way I wanted things. The way I needed them. And really, it seemed a small enough thing to ask for. Especially when you look at all the shit *I* had put up with since rising from the dead. Frankly, if the king of the vampires didn't like it, he could take a flying fuck at a rolling doughnut.

"If you don't like it," I said, "you can take a flying fuck at a rolling doughnut."

"Is that another of your tribe's charming post-ceremony activities?"

"What is this 'my tribe' crapola?" I'd given up on the announcements and had started folding my T-shirts—the basket had been silently condemning me for almost a week. Now I dropped a fresh, clean one so I could put my hands on my hips and *really* give him the glare. "Your dad was a Minnesota farmer, for the love of You-Know-Who."

Sinclair, working at the desk in the corner (in a black suit, on a Tuesday night—it was the equivalent of a guy getting up on his day off and immediately putting on a Kenneth Cole before so much as a bowl of cornflakes) simply shrugged and did not look up. That was his way: to taunt, to make an irritating observation, and then refuse to engage. He swore it was proof of his love: that he'd have killed anyone else months ago.

"I am just so sick of you acting like this wedding thing is all me and has nothing to do with you."

He looked up, but didn't put his pen down. "This wedding thing is all you, and has nothing to do with me."

"Shut *up*! Some moldy old book of dead guys tells you we're married and that's good enough for you?"

"Are we discussing the Book of the Dead, or the"—he made a terrible face, like he was trying to spit out a mouse, and then coughed it out—"Bible?"

"Very funny! Look, I'd just like you to say, just once I'd like to hear, that you're happy we're getting married."

"I am happy," he said, "and we are married."

And around and around we went. I wasn't stupid. I was aware that to the vampires, the Book of the Dead *was* the Bible, and if it said we were consorts and co-regents, then it was a done deal.

But I was a different sort of vampire. I'd managed (I think) to hang on to my humanity. A little, anyway.

And I wanted a "real" wedding. With cake, even if I couldn't eat it. And flowers. And Sinclair slipping a ring on my finger and looking at me like I was the only woman in the universe for him. And me looking understated yet devastating in a smashingly simple wedding gown, looking scrumptious and gorgeous for him. Looking *bridal*.

And my family and friends looking at us and thinking, *now there's couple that will make it, there's a couple that was meant to be.* And Marc having a date and Jessica not being sick anymore. And my baby brother not crying once and my stepmother getting along with everybody and not looking tacky. And Antonia not having a million bitchy remarks about "monkey rituals" and Garrett not showing us how he can eat with his feet. And my folks not fighting and peace being declared in the Middle East just before the fireworks (and doves) went up in the back yard, and everybody finding out that chocolate cured cancer.

Well, what the hell. As long as I was heavily fantasizing, right?